FULL OF GRACE

Forty more days and Nineveh will be overthrown.
Book of Jonah 3:4

Patrick Simon D'Arcy

1

1

Mary was just 28 when she was made engineering director at one of the biggest technology companies in the world. She was a very skilful coder 'exceptional talent', as some would say. This was not surprising. From an early age she had always been considered very smart and capable of achieving a lot in her life. After leaving the family home when she was still a teenager and after some hiccups in choosing her career path, she had finally found her way as a programmer. At that time, programming was considered one of the most basic skills that every person should acquire in order to survive in this world.

She liked it – even more, she probably loved it. When she became passionate about something she enjoyed doing it, was very difficult to stop her. Still, she had difficult moments in her work life. Her patience was pretty much limited to a few minutes. Sometimes she was just like a volcano preparing for a massive eruption. Little sparks could turn on the volcano of emotions in her very quickly, and then nothing could stop it. It was better for everyone to not be around when this happened.

But being a coder was really good for her: there was not much to be mad about. In her first career choice – teaching – there had been many more situations where she just got so annoyed with people and children that it was impossible for her to control it. Maybe she'd realised that and that was why she had changed her profession. Coding and computers were her friends, they didn't annoy her a lot, and they just worked as intended.

She was 29 now and her life was still mostly about work but that was changing slowly. Her husband and child were having a much bigger impact on her life than she had expected.

'Mary! We need to talk,' said a tall, geeky-looking man, stopping Mary in the corridor.

'John, do we have to do it now? I really need to leave the office, so I can catch my train and get home,' Mary replied, rushing through the corridor.

'Yeah, I wanted to talk about this, frankly speaking,' John replied with little confidence, knowing that this one sentence could be the spark that would set the volcano off.

'What the heck do you mean?! Let's sit there.' Mary pointed to some chairs in the corner of the room. They quickly sat down and John started explaining himself. John was a typical representative of the majority of twenty-first-century men. He pretended to be okay with all of this gender equality, but at the same time had huge doubts. It was okay, he guessed, as no one was able to prove that it was otherwise. He truly believed that to be successful you don't have to like the rules; you just need to play by them.

'Well, you leave the office early these days …' he started quietly, like he was ashamed of saying this.

'Yes, I'm … I have some responsibilities at home, people who are important to me, and this is what I have to do these days. Leave the office earlier.' She was surprised herself, that she was still calm as she said this.

'I understand, but what about the projects we are working on? We need your guidance here, because we will not move any further without your reviews and feedback.' John was now more confident in what he wanted to say.

'Listen, I worked my ass off to get to this position, to where I am now. There are always going to be some projects, but I also need to prioritise some other things in my life – family. I'm not getting any younger.' Mary was getting a bit annoyed at this point.

'Yeah, that's what Mark said as well, women will always prioritise their family at some point ...' John said without realising he'd spoken out loud.

'What?! You must be kidding me!' Yep, this was a spark.

'Oh crap. Did I say that out loud?' John felt a bit embarrassed.

'Yes, you did. And I don't appreciate your comment about women's priorities! Listen to me now: this is why I have you on my team, so you can lead projects without my input. So stop whining like a little child and do some useful stuff. See you tomorrow.' Mary got up and rushed to the door. She was almost late for her train. Fortunately, the train would wait for her for another minute or more, because the AI transportation system knew exactly where she was and if she was going to make it.

The whole way back, she kept thinking about this conversation. She was very tired and annoyed by those kinds of situations. It wasn't the first time her ability to do the job had been questioned because of her gender. It was a difficult path all the way up to director level, when at every stage she had to prove herself and prove that she could do the work that men were supposedly meant to be doing. And those assumptions that, because she was a woman, she would do things her own way. She would become a mother one day and not care about work anymore. She was fed up with all of those assumptions. She didn't want to think about this anymore. It was family time. She switched off from work mode. As much as her career was important to her and had been for many years, she had found out that for her, happiness lies somewhere else, in family and healthy relationships with people she cared about.

***

Helen hadn't had a family yet. She was four years younger than Mary. She had long dark hair, slightly red cheeks and blue eyes that were full of happiness – but not as much as they had been when she was a child or even a teenager. Life was hard on her, without a doubt. She was alone, with no realistic prospects of having a family life in the near future. At least she was fulfilling her dreams in her professional life. Like her sister, Mary, her childhood dream had been to become a teacher. And she was one – she was a History teacher at St. John Baptist High School on the Upper East Side in Manhattan. She loved that job – it was really her vocation to teach kids. It was a girls-only high school and most of the teenagers really liked her, too.

She had this easy way of connecting with them, of explaining how historic events influence our society and politics today. She was also very honest with them. The girls trusted her because she hadn't just taught them history but also about life and all its nuances. Teaching history now was very different from before. There was no need to memorise facts, you could find them online in a split second. It varied from country to country but in the US, history focused on events in a logical and chronological sequence. Children were also taught History of Technology and History of Politics and Society, so they could grow up to be engaged and understanding citizens. It was very rare for kids to have to write anything. As for other subjects, instead of Maths there was Programming, and Science was usually taught in an augmented reality environment, so the kids were able to almost be a part of the experiments and touch nature.

On this particular day, Helen finished work a bit earlier. The class that usually had History at 1 p.m. was out that day. They had gone to the science competition. It didn't bother her to leave the school a bit earlier. It was a lovely day in New York City. Sunny, with no clouds at all. A beautiful April day. She picked up her bag, put her sunglasses on and turned on her music player. She wasn't a big fan of listening to music, but New York was a really noisy city and just to focus on her thoughts she had to play some relaxing, quiet music. She put her earphones on and started walking. Helen wasn't much into technology. Her earphones were 'old-school'. No wireless Bluetooth connection. They were really ancient, wired earphones, the kind they had stopped making at least a decade ago. She plugged them into her 2025 music player. It worked well for her, so it was fine.

She chose her standard route home, through Central Park. She went straight up East 75th Street, passed through Lexington Avenue, Park Avenue and then Madison Avenue. Then she turned right onto Fifth Avenue, just so she could enter the park closer to the Alice in Wonderland statue. As usual, she spent a few minutes looking at it, and as always, she was amazed by the artistry of the statue. After the statue she took a right and went in the direction of Bethesda Fountain. It was still early, so there were not many people in the park, at least in this part.

She passed Andersen Statue on her left and turned right to go across East Drive. There was a group of teenagers sitting on a park bench. Mostly boys, maybe 17 to 18 years old. There were five of them. They didn't look like they were missing a day in school … more likely a whole year, or years of school. They were wearing black or grey hoodies and were loud, and drinking something that was definitely not a soft drink. To look at them you could think that men had not changed a bit over the centuries. They were still interested in having power over others, especially women. And their favourite thing to do, which made them very proud of themselves, was doing nothing.

She ignored them at first. Not the first time she was seeing teenage boys sitting on a bench in the park. But they were different. They had been loud, but turned quiet when Helen passed. Helen suddenly felt fear pass through her body like a bolt of lightning from the sky. Her music was pretty quiet so she could hear them, and she decided to leave it like that. She pretended to ignore them and not to be interested. She didn't look at them, in order not to draw attention to herself. They started talking to each other. 'Look at this chick! She looks like a teacher in that dress …'

'Miss, I didn't do my homework. I was a naughty boy. Can you spank me?'

'Yes, you were a very naughty little boy …' another replied, putting on a woman's voice.

'Stop pretending with that gay voice,' shouted the other one. 'Get her to spank you … Maybe she can give you a bit more!' They all started laughing.

One of them, a tall boy with blond hair and blue eyes, got up and started walking towards Helen. She felt him staring at her. She heard his every step on the sandy ground. She was really scared, but she was even more afraid to turn around and look into his face, hidden behind the hoodie.

'Hey you! Beautiful lady,' he shouted and then laughed. Helen ignored him, and continued walking at the same pace.

'Hey, I'm talking to you, bitch!' The teenager started to get a bit annoyed that she hadn't even turned around.

'Leave her alone, she can't hear you,' someone shouted from the bench. Helen's heart was beating very fast. She really wanted to be somewhere else right now.

'Eh … Whatever, anyway.' The blond teenager stopped, turned around and started walking back towards his friends.

Helen was relieved. She sped up so she could get home quicker. She couldn't stop thinking about this incident. When she entered her apartment, she dropped the handbag on the floor and sat down on a chair. She started to cry. She felt like an animal, an object that can be used to satisfy the needs of men. She felt like she was nothing.

In some ways it was incredible that humanity had been able to improve people's lives, giving them opportunities to develop professionally and personally, while at the same time, stereotypes were still a problem, as was thinking about others as objects that could be owned, and treating them without respect. Actually, these things might even have gotten worse. Men could be the bravest fighters for gender equality and at the same time they might be abusing their wives mentally or physically at home, in their private spaces that no one had access to.

***

Simone was just 17 when her parents died in 2030 during the Third World War. A war that had been so different from previous wars. There was no need for millions of soldiers, no need for weapons and bullets. Words could kill even more, and this was what had happened.

It had been a very difficult loss for her. On the outside she was very strong and confident. On the one hand, she knew that she was smart, beautiful and capable of doing whatever she wanted in her life. On the other hand, she was very troubled and confused inside. She had a hard time understanding why her parents had sacrificed their lives and left her alone in this world.

She got pregnant when she was only 19 and got married just a year later. Then she moved to Boston with her spouse and son. This was her escape, from the people closest to her, who reminded her of her family history. It was an escape from herself as well. She forgot about her needs and dreams and fully focused on supporting her husband and raising her child.

Her husband, Marcus, was a lawyer in one of the biggest law firms in Boston. He was a junior partner there with huge opportunities to move up and lead the whole firm one day. He was much taller than Simone, so when they were out walking on the street Simone sometimes looked more like his daughter than his wife. He was very intelligent but also dominant, and with well established thoughts about his values in life. In everyday life he was proud and stubborn. Simone valued him a lot and thought that he was the best thing that had ever happened to her. She had made a conscious decision to dedicate herself to her partner and child years ago, and her boy was now 5 years old – Francis. And this was what she had been doing for the last couple of years: taking care of her family. Even though her marriage was far from ideal, it was decent. No big fights, none at all, really, because Simone was very humble in that area. Maybe that wasn't exactly the right word. She appreciated Marcus for having looked at her and made her his wife. She didn't feel worthy.

That Tuesday wasn't much different from any other day. The weather was pretty good, so Simone decided to take her son to the playground, the usual spot in the middle of Boston. Not many people were around – just some grannies with their grandchildren. In the twenties most mothers had full time jobs and had a babysitter to look after their child. Though that was actually not so common anymore these days, because – it seemed like there were fewer children around, in general. People were busy with their careers. They didn't want to waste their time on children. People who wanted to get pregnant had huge issues actually doing it. Alcohol, drugs and mostly the poor quality food had killed a lot of valuable cells in people's bodies. Fertility treatments were not the best option either, people had realised. After many years of successful treatment, new diseases had been discovered, which were apparently caused by genetic problems. It had been explained on the news that clinics had been using sperm from just a couple of donors to treat many patients. Hundreds, if not thousands of children in some areas of the country, turned out to be siblings and half-siblings. There was also another group of people who just wanted to save the earth. And they came up with this brilliant idea: that not having children would have a positive effect on climate change and the environment. Overall, the result was that there were far fewer children around. Societies were getting older and schools were closing because of the limited number of students.

This had never been an option for Simone. She had been really happy to become a mother and Marcus had also been ready for this change in his life. Simone couldn't imagine having a stranger take care of her child while she was at work. Because she had had Francis so young, she had also never finished high school, so she didn't have a proper education and couldn't actually get a decent job.

She liked this playground. It was not far from her house, in the city centre, but not crowded like the other ones. Not so small, and not big either, so you could easily find your child. There were a few regular kids who came almost every day. Francis was one of them. Simone always appreciated being outside and getting some fresh air. And even though it was in the city centre, it was not at all loud because it was set a little way back from the street. The playground was actually in the middle of the Christopher Columbus Waterfront Park.

'May I take this seat?' asked an older lady who was at the playground with her grandson.

'Of course you can,' Simone responded, making a space on the bench.

'Johnny! Go and play now. I will be sitting right here,' said the granny to the 4-year-old boy. Simone smiled at her and went back to watching her son.

'How is the day going so far? Lovely weather, right?' remarked the older lady.

'Yes, it is really nice today. How are you doing?' Simone responded.

'I feel in my bones that there'll be changes in the weather, but otherwise just great. Johnny, what are you doing?' she shouted at a little boy. Johnny had started to fight with Francis. Simone immediately stood up and started running towards him.

'Franky are you ok? What has this boy done to you?' Simone called her son by his pet name and hugged him.

'What happened here?' the older lady asked as she joined them.

'This boy took my toy!' shouted Johnny.

'I don't think so. You punched him in the face. Look at his face. Is that right Franky?' Simone was a bit angry at the other boy, and she could almost feel her son's pain.

'Yes Mummy. I didn't do anything wrong. He just punched me,' Frank cried.

'I'm sure that Johnny would not hit you for no reason,' explained the granny.

'Maybe you don't know your grandson very well then' Simone responded, very annoyed. She took Frank's hand and started moving towards the bench.

'Excuse me?!' The older lady didn't know if she just had heard right.

'Yeah, you heard me! You should teach your grandson some manners!' shouted Simone.

'And you had better teach your son to tell the truth!' the old lady quickly responded.

Simone quickly left the park with Frank and went home. The little boy had a small mark just beside his right eye.

'Poor little thing,' said Simone, pressing a small bag of ice to the side of his head.

'Hey Simone! You home?' her husband's voice filled the house.

'Yes, we are' Simone responded, filled with fear.

Marcus entered the kitchen, where Simone and Franky were. 'What happened to him?!' Marcus shouted when he saw the bag of ice on the boy's eye.

'Just a small accident,' Simone responded quickly to end the conversation.

'What?' Marcus was getting annoyed.

'The boy at the park hit me,' cried Franky.

'What?! I can't believe this! How could you let this happen?! What kind of mother are you? How can I trust you if you can't take care of your 5-year-old?'

'I don't …' Simone's eyes began to fill with tears.

'Francis, go to the living room and watch some TV,' Marcus said.

'I'm sorry. It won't happen again,' Simone cried.

'It had better not happen again. Because there will be consequences! Give me some dinner,' Marcus commanded. He didn't even pretend that he respected Simone. He tried to take advantage of her whenever he could.

***

Constance was the youngest of the Murphy sisters. In 2037 she was just 20. When their parents had died seven years ago, she had gone to live with Aunt

Vivian – Dad's cousin. Vivian was really the only person willing to accept anyone from this cursed family. All of the other close family, her mother's and father's siblings, hadn't wanted to take the sisters into their homes. They were either afraid of the government or just thought that what happened to their brother and sister in 2030 was actually just. 'Harmful ideas have to be punished before they are released to the public,' they would think to themselves. Even if that meant killing their siblings. Aunt Vivian was not a bad person. She wanted the best for Constance, but she was just not able to give her that. She was almost 50 years old at the time. She was single and living alone in a big house. She had her habits and ways of doing things and was simply not equipped to raise a teenage girl. A teenage girl at the worst possible age.

Her parents had been killed, she'd been separated from her sisters, she was in a new house, new town, new school, with new friends – it was teenage rebellion time. It was a difficult time for Constance and her aunt, who didn't get it, and was just not suitable for the job. Vivian grew angry with Constance because of her attitude and for not being grateful for what she had done for her. At one point she even regretted taking her into her home.

Constance tried everything to rebel against her aunt. Breaking the house rules and not listening to her aunt was just a small part of it. She started to have trouble at school. Fights, terrible grades, drugs – just to name a few. When she was 16 she started running away from home. She would be gone for a few days or even for a few weeks. And then she would always come back for some proper food and a place to sleep.

When she was 18 and finally moved out, Aunt Vivian was relieved. All the new grey hair and regular conversations with school staff and the police had made her really regret the decision she'd made five years earlier. She didn't care where Constance went or what she did. Constance soon dropped out of high school and the troublemaker kid was living on the streets of New York. Not the best place for an 18-year-old, but thanks to her intelligence and ability to survive any situation, she was actually doing pretty well.

'Hey handsome, do you want to play with me?' Constance said to a young, black-haired man who was passing her on the street.

'What?' He didn't get it at first, as he was looking at his brand-new electronic gadget.

'You heard me. Are you interested in tasting this? Free candy?' Constance being very flirty to keep his attention.

'Sure, yeah,' he finally looked at her.

'Come over here.' Constance invited him to follow her into an alley between two shops. He followed her with a smile on his face. You might wonder who would go for something like this. But this was a different generation. People were constantly living in a virtual world and were hungry for real human interaction. They weren't able to rationally assess situations. And there were individuals who knew exactly how to take advantage of that.

Considering that Constance had been living on the streets for a couple of years now, she didn't look bad. She wore stolen clothes and the money she made from dealing drugs made her look pretty decent. She didn't care much about how she looked, but her natural beauty was visible. Dark blond hair, never brushed but always styled so you would think that the greatest hairdressers had done it. She didn't wear much makeup, as she had never liked it. She had enough confidence in herself to think that she didn't need to change anything about her looks. Maybe this was not love, but it was definitely some kind of acceptance of who she was and how she looked.

She pushed the man against the wall and started kissing his neck. When he closed his eyes she quickly removed his golden watch and kicked him in the crotch. He screamed and fell to the ground. Constance ran.

'What the heck? Why? I will get you!' he screamed. It was like waking up from a lovely dream for him. He got up and started running after Constance, but she was very fit so she was fast and could run fast for long distances. She also knew Brooklyn very well, so it was easy for her to hide somewhere in a dark alley. And that was what she did. She turned off from the main street into an alley, then turned right just after passing the most famous bar in Brooklyn, and then turned right again into a closed alley. Her buddies were already waiting for her.

'And here is Conny, what do you have for us?' said the man wearing a red hoodie and black baseball hat.

'Who wants a golden watch?' Constance laughed and showed them the watch she'd stolen.

However, although the man she'd stolen from wasn't the quickest person on earth, he got there eventually.

'I told you I would get you, bitch!' suddenly Constance's victim showed up in the alley.

'Who are you calling a bitch, smart boy?' the man in the red hoodie responded quickly.

'She stole my watch!' the man shouted.

'Do we have a problem, Conny?' the man asked Constance.

'Not my problem. I gotta go.' And Constance ran into the next alley, behind her buddies' backs.

'That's what I thought. Gentlemen, we might have a complaining customer here. How can we deal with this complaint? The man in red hoodie turned around to the group of men.

'We can solve the problem with one punch!' someone shouted from the crowd. Constance's buddies ran towards the man and started punching and kicking him. He could not defend himself – there was only one of him against seven well-built young men. Constance was watching from atop a wall that she had climbed while running away. She didn't enjoy them beating this guy but thought 'Well, what can you do – life can beat you up sometimes for no reason.' Then she walked away.

Four sisters. Nothing in common anymore. Two had even changed their surnames. Different lives, different environments, different values. But that was about to change. And it all started with one page, a piece of paper, a word that had almost been removed from everyone's vocabulary – a letter. A real one, sent via the post.

***

Mary got into her apartment building by opening the door with her phone. The door made a squeaky noise. She passed a line of rusty letterboxes. She didn't even know why they still had them. The last time she'd received a letter via the post had been three years ago. 'What the heck?' she thought. There was a letter in her letterbox. She quickly checked if she still had the key to it. She did. She opened the box and took out the letter. 'Where did this come from?' she thought. No return address. Nothing. Just her name and address.

She started opening the letter as she walked up the stairs. She read the first few sentences and sat down on the stairs. 'What is this all about?' Her heart started to beat faster, in some vague way she felt afraid of what this could be and how it might impact her life. At the same time, she felt herself get excited. An unknown sender, visiting a mysterious place. She always loved to challenge herself to overcome her limits or fears, and this was another chance to do that.

***

The situation at the park had ruined Helen's day. Once she got home she went to bed and stayed there until evening. Later, she got up, had something to eat and went to bed again. She was not really sleeping but instead thinking about what had happened at the park and about her life in general. 'Is there anything to look forward to?' she asked herself. 'Probably not,' she answered herself quickly, feeling nothing. She didn't have much hope. She didn't have anyone who could give her that hope for a better future.

She woke up early the next morning and put some clothes on and decided to get some fresh milk and rolls for breakfast. 'A little moment of happiness,' she thought. This was quite unusual in those days, but there were still some places that actually had those things available for walk-ins from the street. Most of the time, those kinds of products were ordered online automatically, when they began to run low in kitchens.

She opened the door and was surprised to see a letter that had been pushed under the door. 'A letter? Must be the landlord again,' she thought, even though it was very hard for her to imagine a 90-year-old man coming to her door and leaving a letter.

'Weird,' she thought as she looked at the stamp and her name and full address on the letter. 'Usually the landlord would not use the post office to send those,' she thought as she started opening the envelope. She sat on the couch and started reading. A natural, beautiful smile showed up on her face. 'Maybe this day won't be so awful after all,' she said to herself. She left the letter on the couch and went to get something for her breakfast. Amazingly, that letter had changed her mood and given her the hope she was looking for. Like there is always someone listening who knows what we need.

***

'That wasn't so bad,' said Marcus to Simone after finishing his dinner. This was as much of a compliment as she had been able to get from him in the last five years.

'I'm glad you liked it,' Simone responded, without sarcasm – she just heard what she wanted to hear.

'Oh, by the way. There was a letter in the mailbox addressed to you. It is on the table in the living room,' Marcus pointed at the letter.

'Thank you honey. Get some rest now. You must be very tired after a long day at work,' Simone kissed Marcus' forehead.

'You don't even know. You life is pretty easy at home,' Marcus responded quickly. Simone cleaned up after his dinner and went to play with Francis. Later on that evening she mistakenly threw the letter out with the rubbish.

The next morning when Marcus was fixing the cover of the bin, he saw the unopened letter. 'What the hell, Simone? Why did you throw away this letter? Have you even checked what's inside? Maybe there was a cheque from your rich grandmother in there!' he shouted at Simone and handed her the letter.

'I'm really sorry. I didn't mean to.' She took the letter and went to her room. She sat down on her bed and started reading. She felt nothing whatsoever. She left the letter on the bed and went downstairs to help Marcus get ready to leave for work.

'What was the letter all about?' he asked straight away.

'Nothing interesting,' she responded and again focused on some housework she had started doing.

'Has to be something important, if someone bothered to send this via the post,' he gave Simone a questioning look and started to laugh quietly but cheekily.

'Yeah, maybe. There 's going to be some meeting with old friends this weekend in New York. I'm not planning to go,' Simone responded, not even looking at Marcus.

'I think you should go. You've been very grumpy recently. Maybe this will cheer you up.' Marcus felt proud that he was offering so much goodwill to his wife.

'That's very kind, honey. We'll see.' Simone wasn't very interested, she was busy cleaning Marcus' shoes.

***

'I hope you didn't beat this kid to death,' said Constance to the man in the red hoodie.

'He was all right. We just scared him off a bit. This watch will be worth good money,' he smiled. 'Oh, I forgot! Postman was passing by today, and gave me a letter for you,' he took the letter from his hoodie. It was a bit dirty, and had a few drops of blood on it. He handed it to Constance.

'Postman? Letter? For me?' She seemed surprised.

'Yeah, sorry about the blood. It wasn't there originally,' he turned around and left.

'Letter to me? I feel like I'm 5. Bullshit. No one even cares about me anymore,' she thought and threw the letter into the nearest bin without even opening it. Constance felt alone. Once in a while memories would come back to her and she felt anger towards her parents. She was also annoyed that her wider family had seemed to ignore her and eventually forgot that she even existed. But as much as she didn't like this whole situation, she was living on the streets, and she couldn't show her weaknesses.

2

Another beautiful Saturday morning. Helen woke up early as always. There was nothing she liked better than waking up with the sunrise. Sunrise in New York was gorgeous. The sun between the skyscrapers was an astonishing view, so unreal. You could see people crossing the street in the distance, and they were like painted trees on this bloody orange sun that was behind them.

She got out of bed, cleaned her eyes in the bathroom and looked out the window. She smiled and said, 'I have a feeling that this will be a good day.' Helen was always honest with herself. She didn't like to pretend that everything was fine, and keep going. She was lonely. Still, she always tried to be brave and do what was best for her. It was not always easy, but at least she tried.

The trip to Long Island was neither quick nor easy. But self-driving cars made it at least less tiring for drivers. She put on some clothes – not too elegant, but not casual, either. She didn't know what to expect. Her parents' old house. The one where she had spent all of her childhood. She was not even sure if the house was empty or if maybe someone was living there. That chapter of her life was meant to be closed and pretty well sealed, at least that was what her family and government wanted. In reality, her heart could never forget her parents and life with them. No one could erase all of those memories. She

requested a self-driving taxi and grabbed some
bagels to take with her. When she got downstairs,
the taxi was already waiting. The door opened itself.
She got in.

'Good morning Helen, where would you like to go
today?' asked the voice in the car. 'To Long Island?'
it asked in the follow-up question.

'Yes. Please bring me to Long Island, Hill Drive,'
she responded, and started eating the bagel. In some
ways it was scary that those machines knew so much
about people and their lives, but at the same time it
was very helpful to everyone, so people accepted it.

'Of course, Helen. The trip should not take longer
than 50 minutes. Let me know if you want to listen to
music, the news or if you have any other questions.
Please buckle your seatbelt,' the car assistant added.

'Done. Let's go for a ride,' Helen said with a note of
excitement in her voice.

Helen loved New York City. She had moved here
when she was little. Her parents had emigrated from
Ireland in 2017, when she was only 5. She called
herself a 'New Yorker'. This was really what she
knew. She could not remember much about Dublin.
She had never visited Dublin again. New York was a
city made for her. It was noisy and busy, but it was
also easy to separate yourself from it and be lonely if
you needed to. There were loads of different places
where you could meet with your friends for something
to eat or drink. It was filled with beautiful parks, huge
bridges and water. All in all, it was a great place to
live. The diversity of people and cultures living there
was astonishing. You could see the influence of

every culture in the world somewhere in New York City. The city had not always been pleasant to her; she had some bad memories related to some parts of New York, but she tried not to think of them too often.

Long Island was not one of those places. The Murphy family had lived there until they were split up after her parents' death seven years ago. As she had been very close with her family, she had only good memories of that time. The worst one was really when her parents had died and the sisters had been split up.

It was 8:25 a.m. She had reached her final destination: Hill Drive, Long Island. 'Is there anything else I can do for you today Helen?' the car assistant suddenly started to talk.

'No, thank you,' Helen responded.

'Thank you for using our service. Have a great day Helen!' The doors opened and Helen got out of the car. She was there. Standing on her old street, where she could remember riding a bike for the first time and playing soccer with the neighbourhood kids. She saw her parents' house in the distance. She felt a bit nervous for a second, but then started to walk towards the meeting place, as described in the letter.

***

Simone had a longer distance to travel to get to Long Island by 10 a.m. on Saturday. But these days it was not a huge problem. The Hyperloop had never been rebuilt after the Third World War in 2030, but there were electric planes and super-fast trains.

Simone had never really left her child for so long. It wasn't even for such a long time now, either. Just a few hours really. Still, she was scared how Franky would survive this time without her.

'Don't worry. I will take care of him. Do what you have to do,' Marcus tried to reassure Simone, thinking that maybe her trip would benefit him as well.

'Thank you honey, you are so kind.' Simone wasn't convinced but she decided to go. 'Maybe it will be good for them, so they can get a break from me for a few hours,' she thought.

She took a plane at 7 a.m. from Logan airport and landed in JFK around 8 a.m. For some reason this was a very busy day at the airport. It was the weekend and the weather was lovely, the best time to visit New York City. That definitely didn't help with the traffic around the airport. Even with all of the technology, self-driving cars and super-fast trains, if one hundred thousand people wanted to leave the airport at the same time, there was no way to avoid traffic jams. Finally, after a slow twenty-minute drive to the highway she was able to speed up the self-driving ride.

She got to Connetquot Park just after 9 a.m. Why the park? Because it was close to the house, and Simone decided she wanted to take a walk through the park. There were great views, the river, some wild animals even. And there were memories. Her parents' death was still really painful for her, though she tried to hide it well. Her defence mechanism was to escape, to avoid thinking about it and just let everything go, the good and the bad memories together.

All of that was buried inside her. The only thing that was left were the good memories of times when they had played in this park; Mum, Dad and her sisters. The Sunday walk after church and before dinner was a family tradition. She wanted to spend some time here, to listen to the birds and see the spring waking nature from its winter sleep. She wanted to quiet her emotions as well. She was still thinking about Franky and Marcus. She had already rung them three times since she had left the house. The other thing was the house. The old family house, full of pain and bad memories. And she didn't even know why she was here, and why she was going there.
'Ok, Simone, pull yourself together, focus and go,' she told herself to motivate herself to walk up the final path that led to Hill Drive, where the house was.

***

Constance opened her eyes. 'Where am I?' she thought, lying in a king-size bed, staring at the ceiling. She jumped out of bed and opened the curtains. 'Wow, that's really shitty taste,' she thought when she saw the red covers with the Manchester United logo. She looked around, found a marker and started writing huge capital letters on the white wall: YNWA. 'Yep, now it's better,' she said to herself, smiling.

But she still didn't know where she was. It was not her house, as she didn't have one. And most of her buddies from the street didn't really have a place to stay, either. So that was something new to her. The room looked like it belonged to a little boy. 'Maybe not so little,' Constance thought when she saw shaving foam in the bathroom.

'Crap, I hope I didn't break into this house,' she said out loud.

'She didn't have to put on clothes, or shoes, for that matter, because it didn't look like she had taken anything off the previous night. She went downstairs, took a quick tour but still didn't really recognise the place. She just found loads of empty bottles, dirty dishes, and empty crisp packets.

'The party was definitely successful, but why is there no one here?' she thought. 'I had better go now. Oh, my head.' Constance grabbed her head, then started checking the kitchen drawers for painkillers. She found some, swallowed them and had a glass of water. 'I guess it's time to go now.' She left the glass in the kitchen sink and went straight to the front door. It was open, so she just let herself out and shut it behind her. Then she went straight through the front garden to the street.

'Ok, that's no better. I still have no idea where I am. Looks kind of familiar though … not like Brooklyn, but I have a feeling that I was here before,' Constance was talking to herself and turned left onto the sidewalk. She was exploring her surroundings, trying to figure out where she was. Everything was kind of familiar to her, but she didn't know why. Finally she got to a junction. The sign on the corner said Hill Drive, Long Island.

'No way. How the hell have I ended up here? That's miles away from Brooklyn. Sounds like I will have an exciting trip back to town,' she thought. 'Wait a minute, our old house was somewhere here. This is why this all is so familiar.' She started thinking. 'That way.' She turned right and started walking straight up Hill Drive.

***

Mary was very excited to visit the old family house in Long Island. She didn't know if her parents and sisters were still living there. It didn't look like the letter had been written by one of them. Even if there was nothing interesting there, just an empty house, it was enough for her to be excited to come back to the place she'd spent her whole childhood in.

It was almost ten years ago now that she had had a fight with her parents and moved out. She had never called them again, or visited her sisters or anything. She'd burned that bridge. Now she didn't even remember why she had moved out. She was just 19 at the time, it had probably just been her temperament and character: independent and stubborn. Now that she had a family, a husband and child, she looked at things from a different perspective. She was really keen to talk to her mum, and to see how she handled problems in the family. Recently she had started to think about what her sisters' lives looked like. Maybe they had families, maybe not. Maybe they were famous. She was very interested in knowing how her little sisters were doing. Maybe it was just curiosity or maybe she was missing them and wanted to chat.

'Honey!' Mary said to her husband. 'I will have to go now, just for a few hours. In thirty minutes Mrs

O'Brien should come over to help you with the house and John.'

John, her 7-year-old son, whom they had adopted a year earlier, was still asleep. Mary went to his room, gave him a kiss on the cheek and tucked him in. It was 7 a.m. when she left the apartment and went to her car. She wanted to beat the New York City traffic and this was the only chance to do it.

In spite of how up-to-date Mary was with technology, there was one thing she couldn't give up: driving a car. She just loved it. Self-driving cars were not an option for her. She had to feel the ride, be in control. She didn't want to give the computer an opportunity to decide how to drive and at what speed. Sometimes she just drove for fun, or to calm down. Yes, driving was like a medicine for her boiling emotions and something that focused her attention so quickly and effectively that it was the only solution in moments of troubled depression. A twenty-first century disease: depression. People had high expectations for themselves as well as others. And they were not able to cope with them, because as much as we would like for this not to be the case, we are weak, vulnerable and will disappoint ourselves and others. That is the beauty of being a human.

She drove a few good rounds on Long Island. She hadn't been here for a long time. She still had so many good childhood memories, and stories related to this place when she was a teenager. She was smiling every few minutes as she passed places and corners where she remembered something good and pleasant happening to her when she was young.

She got to the house around 9 a.m. and parked the car on the street. She got out of her Lexus and walked directly to the house. The porch was on the left. There was an old wooden bench there, and someone was sitting on it.

***

'Good Morning' said Mary to the girl in the dark red dress who was sitting on the bench. The girl turned around and smiled cheerfully.

'Mary?' Tears of happiness ran down her cheeks. Helen's heart started to beat much quicker.

'Helen! So good to see you!' Mary shouted and hugged her. She was surprised but very excited to meet her younger sister.

'Many years have passed! I'm so glad to see you, Mary!' Helen was very happy to see her.

'Are you still living here?' Mary asked, smiling.

'Oh no. This house has been empty for quite a long time. I just got a letter …'

'A letter, you say?' Mary interrupted her. 'I got one as well,' she added.

'Yeah, that's actually interesting,' Helen started thinking about who could have sent them both a letter.

'How are you doing?' Mary asked, not knowing how to continue the conversation.

'I'm doing great. How are things with you Mary? It's been a while since I last saw you. Since before … probably a few years before this awful war,' Helen said.

'Yes, I guess it has been too long. I was thinking about you the other day. I wanted to come back and make peace with our parents. Yeah, how are they doing?' Mary continued.

'Oh, you don't know,' Helen felt a bit ashamed.

'Don't know about what?' Mary asked.

'They died, or rather, they were killed in the war seven years ago.' Helen put her head down. Mary looked at the house and went quiet. She didn't say anything. Probably hundreds of thoughts were going through her head at that moment.

'Not sure what to say …' A tear ran down Mary's face.

'I'm sorry, we didn't say anything. We just couldn't find you.' Helen felt even more ashamed

'No. It is not your fault. I didn't want to be found,' Mary responded.

Helen turned to look at the street and saw a girl staring at the house.

'Is that not Constance?' Helen asked Mary. Mary turned around.

'I don't know if I would recognise her …' Mary said, feeling a bit embarrassed.

'Constance!' Helen shouted.

'Oh shit, someone is here …' Constance said to herself when she noticed the person shouting at her. She started walking and pretending that she didn't know them.

'I think it's her. Maybe she didn't hear,' Helen said to Mary and started running towards her youngest sister.

'Constance, is that you?' she shouted again. Helen got closer and put a hand on her shoulder. Constance turned around.

'It is you, right?' Helen asked hesitantly

'Yes, I guess so. And you are?' Constance seemed surprised by the whole situation.

'Helen, I'm Helen, your sister,' Helen looked into her eyes and hugged her.

'Oh, it's been a long time,' Constance responded emotionlessly, like she didn't care.

'Yes, don't you recognise me?' Helen asked.

'Yeah, maybe, no, not really,' Constance responded.

'Mary is here as well,' Helen said and waved to Mary for her to come over. Mary quickly moved to the pavement outside the house.

'Hi, little sister,' Mary said, and kissed Constance on the cheek.

'Mary, right. Big sister, who left us.' Constance said it with a hint of disappointment. She had not expected that meeting and she definitely didn't feel like speaking to her sister just then.

'Yeah. Did you get a letter as well?' Mary asked.

'Letter? No I was just drinki…yeah, I got a letter.' Constance stopped herself and decided not to tell the full story, which she couldn't even remember. Then she realised that she actually had got the letter, but thrown it away.

'I haven't heard from you in quite a long time now. I heard some stories from Aunt Vivian when you were living with her. Was everything alright?' Helen looked concerned.

'I'm just fine. Managing my life the way I want. Poor Aunt Vivian didn't always get that,' she winked at Helen.

'Alright. So what are you doing now?' Helen continued.

'Yeah, just messing around. Nothing major,' Constance replied quickly.

'Why were you living with Aunt Vivian?' Mary chimed in.

'When our parents died, they had to split us between family and friends. Not everyone wanted to take us. They were afraid of the government and that our genes would force us to grow into the same evil people as Mum and Dad, with those politically incorrect views on life,' said Constance with confidence. Mary was a bit confused, she wasn't really getting the whole background. At the same time, she started to feel guilty. As the grown-up sister at the time, she could actually have been their guardian.

'Sorry to hear that,' she responded, looking guilty.

'I'm sorry too. Or maybe not anymore. I guess it doesn't matter now. Listen, I have to go now. It was nice to chat, but I have some stuff to do,' Constance said and started moving away.

'What?' Helen sounded surprised. 'If you got the letter, that means that you are here for a reason. Let's wait until 10 a.m. and enter the house,' Helen replied.

'Crap, this letter, I forgot' Constance said to herself.

'Yeah, sure, I'll wait until 10 a.m.,' she replied to Helen.

'Is that not Simone coming our way as well?' Mary asked, looking over Helen's shoulder.

'I think it is!' Helen turned around and looked even happier.

'Simone was walking down the street looking around at the houses and after a few seconds she realised that she was being watched. One of the faces looked very happy, the other two not much so.

'Simone! So good to see you!' Helen shouted when Simone was just a few metres away.

'Oh my God. All my sisters. I didn't expect this. So long since I last saw you,' Simone started hugging each of them.

'How are things, my dear sisters? You've changed a bit! You've grown up. And Mary, I have not seen you for years, how have you been? And little Constance is not so little anymore.' Simone was excited to see them.

'I'm glad you remember my name,' Constance said quietly, her body language making it clear how much she didn't want to be there.

'How have you been, Simone?' Helen asked.

'Grand, I guess. Married, have a son. Living in Boston.'

'So you came over from Boston? Wow, that's a pretty long journey I guess,' Mary looked amazed by this effort.

'Ok. It is almost 10 a.m. now. I suggest we go inside, like we were told to in the letter,' Helen said and started leading her sisters to the entrance.

'Oh, so you all got the letter as well,' Simone remarked. 'That's very interesting. I'm wondering who sent them.'

'Let's find out if the answer is inside the house,' Mary said and followed Helen.

'I hope that the front doors are open. I don't have keys,' Helen said, slowly walking towards the entrance.

'I guess, it would be nice to get inside,' added Simone.

'Oh no, it's locked,' said Helen, after trying to open the door.

'What are we going to do now?' Mary asked.

'So I came here for nothing.' Simone sounded disappointed, because she was thinking of the expectations that Marcus had.

'Not for nothing, I'm glad we are all together again. This is a really happy day,' Helen responded, looking into Simone's eyes. Helen had not been so cheerful since the last time the whole family had been together at Christmas.

'Chill out, ladies. Let me have a look,' Constance said in a relaxed manner, with bubble gum in her mouth. She moved towards the door. She checked the handle, took some metal clips from her pocket and tried to insert them into the lock.

'Click! Sorted!' Constance shouted happily and entered first.

'Wow, this place hasn't changed much. It looks like it did when we left it seven years ago,' Constance said, looking around. It was a surprising thing to say for someone who didn't care and at the same time, remembered many details about the old house.

The rest of the Murphy sisters entered the house.

'That's crazy. It feels like the day we left,' Helen added.

'Yep, they didn't even empty the fridge. Everything is green and mouldy. Disgusting …' Constance looked into the refrigerator.

'Close that fridge, Constance! It smells terrible. Are you hungry? Did you get any breakfast?' Helen asked,

'Yeah, not really, I was busy this morning,' Constance replied.

'Have you taken a shower?' Helen asked as she passed Constance and smelled how not fresh she was. 'Or were you too busy for that, as well?' Helen added, smelling not only a lack of showering but bigger issues in Conny's life.

'Yeah, very funny, Helen.' Helen smiled. 'I washed … my face,' Constance said quietly.

'Okay … so let's check what the instructions in the letter were,' Mary said as she took the letter from her pocket and started reading. 'When you enter the house, don't spend much time looking around, just go directly to the attic. There will be an old couch there. Sit on it and wait.' Mary stopped reading.

'Let's do that, then,' Simone said. 'Oh, and here is my room,' Simone was now standing at the door of her old bedroom..

'We have to go to the attic now. We'll come back here.' Simone started walking up the stairs.

'I don't remember ever going up to the attic,' Mary said

'Me neither, Mum was always saying that Dad kept his stuff and there was nothing for us to play with

there,' Simone added, exhibiting a great memory –
or maybe this is just what kids remember when
something is forbidden to them.

The stairs were old and kind of crunchy when you
walked on them. Mary got to the door first. It wasn't
locked. She grabbed the handle and pushed the door
open. The noise of the squeaky door was pretty loud
and annoying to their ears but Mary tried to do it
quickly.

'Wow, it looks like it was Dad's office. Couch, desk,
even little whisky bar. He was into those Irish
whiskeys a lot, I remember.' Simone tried to recall
some memories of her father.

'Is there anything left?' Constance asked, looking at
the minibar.

'Really, Constance?' Helen couldn't believe what
she was hearing. 'It is just 10 a.m., you drink coffee
at that time, not whiskey.' Helen was growing more
and more interested in what had happened to her
little sister. She felt that something was not right.

'Let's sit on the couch and see what happens,'
Mary said, which seemed to be the most reasonable
thing to do at that point.

'Weird, it is not even dusty, like downstairs.
Someone was here not so long ago,' Simone said, as
she sat down on the dark red couch.

All four sisters sat down on the large couch. They
started looking around and got a bit quiet. There
were a lot of thoughts and memories flooding their
minds and hearts at that point. There was a bit of
excitement, because they had no idea what might
happen here. At the same time, this place reminded

them of their happy family times. So it was touching. Some of them tried not to express any feelings, or maybe to escape them, because they were afraid of how they would react.

'Nothing is going to happen here. Bullshit!' Constance stood up after two minutes of silence, which had been killing her inside. She hated it, because too many thoughts were coming to her head. She needed a quick distraction.

'Stop. Give it another three minutes,' Helen replied, and held her hand and asked her to sit again, looking into her eyes the whole time. She was still trying to figure out in her mind what was happening in Constance's life and why she was behaving that way.

'They sat for another three minutes and their minds started to calm down because of the silence and peace that was felt in this attic.

'You are very welcome here!' A male voice spoke and frightened the sisters, so much so that Simone and Mary almost jumped off the couch.

'Hello,' Helen responded.

'We all know that the world is not a perfect place. Human beings try to destroy it, and then rebuild it and try to improve life.' The voice paused for a moment.

'We are living in a beautifully created world. When we travel outside of our cities, we can see breathtaking views. Lakes in the middle of snowy mountains, sunsets over the ocean, rivers going through wild forests. Every day we see less and less of this, though, because we humans need space and resources to live. Still, it is there, it exists and gives us that incredible feeling of the presence of someone, of whoever created this. And we, human beings, were created as well.. So creative, so passionate, intelligent. We are capable of extraordinary things in this world, in our lives. And we do it. Technology and medicine are the best examples of this, where we have reached an incredible level of knowledge. We have automated all repetitive tasks so that humanity can focus on more innovative tasks. We can cure people of diseases we didn't know how to cure just ten years ago. With AI and machine learning we are moving forward in almost every field very quickly.

'Of course there are some disadvantages to this state. We feel invincible, powerful. We think that we can do whatever we want, that we are unstoppable in our development of science. This is why we created a set of rules called 'human rights', to define what it means to be a 'real human being'. It defines the boundaries of our freedom. We have defined what is good and bad for us. We have decided what will help humanity and what will not. And unfortunately this is where the problems began. We are human beings, only human beings. We can't forget about this. We did not create this world. Even with the current state of medicine, where we can create people – it was not like this before. It is not how the world and nature were designed. And we should always remember, that human rights, rules for all humanity, the definition of good and evil, were created by people. Weak people, like you and me. Biased people, who like some things and hate others. People who look at things through the perspective of their own success, or the benefit of their social group. We have replaced real happiness with short-term satisfaction and pleasure. The world is moving too fast to wait for true happiness, which takes too much effort.

'We have removed God, or any type of Creator or religion from our lives. We've replaced it with the religion of humans, where we worship only our needs, our pleasure and our so-called self-development. We are all smart, we know exactly what is best for our environment and we are slowly killing it, and replacing it with technology-based 'nature'. We are so intelligent that we don't need any authorities to tell us how to live our lives – we just need life coaches who will give us a book, written by themselves, with a set of rules about how to be more efficient in our daily productivity. To make humans more useful for the world, themselves and other people. We justify everything with science, knowledge, freedom and dignity, and we let people kill others, kill themselves.

'We say that everything that makes us happy, that gives us this short-term satisfaction, is allowed, even if years ago we said that those same things were so evil and that this wasn't the original plan of our Creator. We are living in a world without any moral rules, without any deep understanding of what love, life, morality, good and evil are all about. We have no time for thinking. It is inefficient to spend time on understanding ourselves. If AI can do it, it means that it is not worth looking into. We are living in a world where a group of people, corporations, decide the course of this world, the course of the whole of humanity. They have full access to our knowledge, to our lives.

'Even more importantly, not accepting this state, not agreeing with this path and that way of understanding is against the set of rules created by those groups. It is against human freedom to disagree with the definition of good and evil. And when you are against this so-called free human development, you can be silenced, you will be punished one way or another.'

The male voice paused, like he was trying to give them time to think about what they had heard.

'Maybe you are thinking now: why should I care? What does this have to do with me? Actually, it has a lot to do with you. Your parents sacrificed their lives for this. They sacrificed their lives because they wanted to find real truth and happiness. They lost their lives alongside many others like them. They were removed from society because they were a sign of opposition. And you have the same feelings in your hearts, the same approach to these problems. Something has been seeded in your souls. The seed of true love and happiness, and a passion for searching for and discovering the truth about yourself and the world.' The voice paused again for a shorter time.

'I need your help. Humanity needs your help. Only the four of you can do something about this. In your rooms you will find letters, addressed to each of the four of you. Those letters will describe your missions. It won't be easy, you might not see results quickly, maybe you won't even see any at all. But just believe and trust. You are not alone, never have been, never will be.'

The Murphy sisters looked astonished. After a minute of silence, Simone said: 'Okay, that was weird. I think we should go home.'

'Wait, wait!' Constance stopped her. 'At least let's go and read the letters. I know that this might just be a stupid joke, but at least it will be something new, there might be something in it for us, at least a reason to get out of bed.'

'Are you saying that you have no reason to get out of bed tomorrow?' Helen asked, curiously, as this confirmed her earlier thoughts about Constance.

'No … sure I have,' Constance responded quickly, but she wasn't convincing anyone.

'What if this is just a set-up from some internal government agency? How does this actually work? Whose voice was that?' Mary stood up and started searching for a speaker.

'Yeah, I don't care. I'm going to my room to read this letter,' Constance replied and left the attic.

Constance's room was the smallest. It was the first on the right side when you got down from the attic. She opened the door. The same bed, the same desk, the same tiny room in the same state as she remembered leaving it seven years ago. She didn't look around even for a bit, she saw the envelope on the bed and went straight to pick it up. She opened the envelope and started reading the letter quickly. She was very curious what it would say. She was done reading in just a few minutes. The letter was not

too long. She looked a bit disappointed, or at least a
bit confused. She started reading again, this time out
loud, just to make sure that she had understood it
correctly:

Dear Constance,

*Your mission is to get together different non-profit
organisations that are fighting amongst themselves
and try to make peace between them. They need to
start talking to each other, at least. Below you will
find a list of organisations, their profiles and their
issues.*

Constance quieted down and read the list again.
There were also names and contact details.
   'Wow. That sounds freaking impossible,' she said
to herself. 'How do they expect me to get there?'
   'Here you go,' Constance found an old debit card in
the envelope. It had a note on it saying that it was
'For expenses'. 'They had thought of everything. Do
those cards even work anymore?' she thought.
   'This is definitely some scam,' she smiled to
herself. She didn't trust that this was a real thing. She
had lost the ability to trust anyone in this world a long
time ago. This was nonsense to her. And she hoped
to get away from there as soon as she could.
   Simone and Helen came down next. They had
shared a room, so they went to the same room
together. Their school portrait from primary school
was still on the wall.

'Oh, I remember when we were that cute and small,' said Helen as she looked around the room. Simone didn't respond. She just grabbed the envelope, opened it and started reading. After a minute, Helen did the same.

'So what is your mission, Sis?' Simone asked.

'Join a school for rich politicians' kids and teach them,' Helen responded.

'Are you happy with that?' Simone asked again, looking at Helen's face. Momentarily Helen looked at her, and remembered that Simone had used to say that every Christmas when they were unwrapping presents.

'I don't know. Not sure what I was expecting. I'm a teacher so this should be doable. What about you?' Helen asked.

'In a nutshell – to figure out how tech companies influence people and what employees think about that. There is the name of a guy who works in one of the branches of a tech company in Cambridge, Massachusetts.

'Doesn't sound bad either. Let's see what Conny and Mary got.' Helen said and they left the room. At the same time, they found Mary standing in the door of her old room with the letter in her hands.

'Did you keep sharing a room after I left?' Mary asked Simone and Helen.

'Yes, Dad never wanted us to move into your room as he always hoped that you would come back,' Helen responded. Tears welled in Mary's eyes. The room looked exactly the way she had left it. She was really sad. The last time she had seen them they had argued about stupid things. And now she knew that she wouldn't see them again. She wouldn't be able to apologise or tell them she loved them anymore.

'So what do you have to do, ladies?' Conny came out of her small room and asked loudly.

'Convince some executives at the United Nations to not change any more laws,' Mary responded quickly.

'Teaching teenagers,' Helen chimed in.

'Infiltrating a tech company,' Simone added.

'Nice, I hope it's not my company,' Mary winked at Simone.

'And I'm going to Europe,' said Constance, smiling. 'Overall, I think it is all bullshit. But at least I got some cash and can travel, so I'll enjoy it.'

The sisters went down to the living room and looked around again.

'So, what now?' Helen asked, hoping that they would grab some lunch and spend some time together catching up. She was so happy to see them again that she did not want to leave them.

'Yeah, I have to go now, I have things to do,' Constance said and left the house. Helen ran after her to the door and shouted: 'What about your mission?'

'Yeah, not sure. I'm crazy, but not that much,' Conny responded.

'Maybe just do it for our parents? Listen, here is my phone number, call me when you need to …'   Helen quickly wrote the number on a piece of paper.

'Yeah, sure. Thanks Helen.' Constance looked into Helen's honest eyes and kind of felt pity for her. She thought that she was so naive that she could count on her. Helen hugged her and Constance left. Helen felt a bit disappointed, but she understood as well that Conny was the youngest and had likely been affected the most by the loss of their parents. And as much as she wanted to help her, to fix her issues, she knew that this would be pointless until Conny realised herself that she needed that help.

'I suggest we get some lunch now. Are you free? What time is your flight, Simone?' Helen asked after returning to the house.

'Not until late afternoon,' Simone responded.

'Let's go then,' Mary smiled and they left the house.

3

Mary, Helen and Simone walked to a small coffee shop that was three blocks from their old house.

'I can't believe that this coffee shop is still here,' said Mary.

'Yeah, I remember how we used to come here when we were children, with Mum and Dad,' added Helen.

'Sunday afternoon treat. Happy times. Even I remember,' pointed out Simone.
They went in through the old wooden door. There was a little bell hanging on the door that announced their arrival. They sat down on rusty chairs.

'I'm so hungry. I could kill for a nice slice of smoked salmon,' said Mary.

'That's funny. That's exactly what Mum used to say,' interrupted Helen.

'Mum really liked salmon, right?' added Simone.

Mary smiled briefly, realising how similar she was to her mother, but the smile passed very quickly because she remembered that it was also her fault that her mother was not there anymore.

'What about you, Helen?' asked Mary, trying to shift the focus away from herself. 'Is there anything you eat that our parents did?'

'Probably sweets,' smiled Helen.

'Yeah, I remember. Mum and Dad could not resist a nice piece of chocolate or cake. And Mum's cheesecake with chocolate on top was just the most delicious cake in the world,' added Simone. Mary went quiet for a moment. She looked at the wall with a different expression on her face.

'Is everything ok, Mary?' asked Helen. Mary didn't respond. Simone touched her hand. 'Cheer up, Sis!' Mary had tears in her eyes.

'Yeah, it is not easy to cheer up. I'm glad to see you again, but at the same time I feel so bad, and responsible that we are here alone, without Mum and Dad,' Mary cried out.

'It's not your fault,' said Simone.

'Yeah, not directly. But they were fighting for their values. They died because of their beliefs. And my beliefs at the time were the opposite. They were the same as those of the people who killed them. Exactly the same. I argued with Mum and Dad. I moved out. And I left you!' Mary was now sobbing.

'It was a rough time for all of us. I'm sure that Mum and Dad were never angry at you. Dad was always saying that he didn't want to give us the answers to every question, because those are always going to be marked with our own views and experiences. And because of that, this truth will never be exactly right, marked with our weaknesses. Dad was sure that every one of us would find the answers, the right answers, but at the right time. Maybe that time is now,' Helen said as she stood up and hugged Mary.

'Let's order something,' Helen said. They all stood up and went to the counter to order some food. After a few minutes they came back and sat in silence for a moment, trying to recall what the voice in the attic had said to them.

Their parents had had very conservative views. Nicholas Murphy was an Irish immigrant born in the 1980s. He'd moved to New York City to continue his studies just at the beginning of the twenty-first century. He witnessed the World Trade Centre collapsing and saw all the weird things that happened in US politics, like the wars in Afghanistan and Iraq. He graduated from New York University. He had a degree in Religious Studies and History.

He had been raised in a Catholic family with views that had been very unpopular at the time, not to mention these days. Throughout his youth, he had tried to reconcile those views and what he believed in with the views the rest of the world had. He was trying to understand how to live a good life, how to become a really good person. He always felt that there was a deeper goodness in every human being, in this world. But the world tries to do only easy good deeds. Good deeds that come from human need only, rather than deeper, existential need, which was designed and seeded in our hearts by God. He lived a secret life, very quiet, often dedicated to contemplative prayer. Though his thoughts and views were very conservative, he never tried to convince anyone to take them on. He always believed that God could do that job Himself, and the job was not to convert people, just love them and live an exemplary life of faith. He tried to teach the same to his daughters. It wasn't easy, because of his approach. He wanted to give them a lot of freedom. He didn't want to convince them, he wanted them to ask the right questions and find the right answers themselves. And the way in which he, his wife and family were living their life was meant to be the answer, meant to be the example. He met his future wife and mother of his four daughters, Barb, when he was studying at NYU. She was just one year younger and was studying Music Theory at the time. She was also an immigrant, having come to New York City from Poland.

They met during an NYU Catholic prayer group meeting. They fell in love, started dating and got married pretty quickly. They were very confident that this was the way to go. When they graduated, and found good enough jobs, they decided to start a family, and in 2008 Mary was born. Of course it wasn't always easy for them. At the beginning of their relationship, when the bond wasn't so strong and deep yet, they argued. When Mary was born, it took them a while to define their priorities and work out a few things. But they loved each other very much, and love overcame all of those differences eventually.

Barbara Murphy was a family person, outgoing and open to other people. After her second child was born, she decided to stay home so she could raise their children. And she didn't really go back to work until the youngest, Conny, was 8 years old.

She was a lovely, good person, always willing to help everyone. Nick always said that she was the better half in their marriage. And sometimes it even looked like she was in charge of the family. Barb was very supportive and without her, Nick would probably have given up many times before 2030. She believed in the same way that he believed. She believed in his mission to give to the world and stand up for his beliefs. She was his rock, on which he built himself and his family. She was very passionate about helping others. This was despite her unpopular views. Most people would remember her for that unconditional love and desire to help everyone.

'And what do you think about the voice in the attic?' Helen suddenly asked. 'With all of that technology around, it is really difficult to distinguish between what is real and what is fake.'

'What do you mean, Helen? Do you really think that could have been Dad's voice out there?' asked Mary.

'Yeah! Maybe he recorded himself before he passed away.' Helen sounded convinced of this idea. She wanted it to be true. For a short time, she had felt again like she was not alone in this world.

'Yeah, I don't know. Possibly, but it is more likely that the FBI created an AI tool to play with us. I know this stuff, I created some of that technology,' Mary responded.

'So what do you do for a living?' Simone asked, not believing what Mary was saying.

'I'm an engineering director at a tech company,' she responded proudly.

'Wow, that sounds impressive,' Simone felt herself getting excited.

'Yes and no. I love my job, but then there are some ongoing challenges that annoy me once in a while.'

'What about the government job you mentioned?' Helen asked.

'Well, I didn't mean that I'm working for a government, but I know that they are using technology, AI voice technology, which I've also created.'

'So do you think that the FBI could be behind all of this, Mary?' Helen asked.

'I don't know what to think. If they are behind it, we might be in trouble. And I have enough trouble myself, not sure if I need more.'

'That doesn't sound like the Mary I knew,' Helen responded, surprised by herself. It was one of those thoughts you think you didn't say out loud but you actually did.

'I have a family now, and I need to take care of them. Simone what do you think? What do you think about the voice?' Mary asked Simone directly, a bit more aggressively.

'I miss my son,' said Simone quietly, like she had not even noticed the higher pitch of Mary's voice.

'How old is he? What is his name?' Helen asked.

'Francis, he is just 5 years old.'

'Tell me more about him.' Helen was curious.

'He's just great. Maybe I'm saying this because he is my only child, but I just adore him. He's a pretty calm boy, he doesn't fight with other kids, like you know boys at that age do. He is very smart, already counts to hundred and writes a few letters. I think he is very different from other boys I have seen on the playground. I know, I sound like a perfect mother with a perfect child.' Her answer couldn't be any different. Like all mothers she saw no weak spots in Francis' personality or behaviour.

'You just love him, that's great. I'm so happy for you,' responded Helen who was genuinely happy when others were, and was able to adjust quickly when they were upset, as well.

'Are you planning on having another child?' Mary asked, out of the blue.

'Yeah, I don't know, really. I think we are happy with one. Maybe in the future. Marcus is very busy at the moment. I don't want to distract him with such matters.'

One might be surprised by such a bold question. Not everyone today has the guts to ask a question like that. And there are many valid reasons for that. It's entering into someone's personal space, which could for some people be too intimidating. But the Murphy sisters were taught to be open, and to separate their emotions from reality. They tried to not feel, just to move on with situations or these types of questions.

'Who is Marcus? I guess he is your partner, apologies … we have not seen each other for so long, I feel that I don't know you at all,' Mary reflected.

'Yes, Marcus is my husband,' Simone answered.

'What does he do?' Helen asked and looked at Simone to see if there was an 'allergic' reaction.

'He is a junior partner in one of the biggest law firms in Boston.'

'Wow, that sounds amazing.' Mary was impressed.

'Yes, he is a very smart man. He got promoted just recently. His hard work has paid off. But this is why he's pretty busy these days. Spending more time at work than at home,' Simone responded with a bit of sadness.

'How do you feel about that?' Helen asked curiously, already knowing the answer to that question.

'I do understand that he has to work. I'm not doing much. Barely anything. Just raising a child and taking care of our home. I don't have a good education. I'm lucky that he actually looked at me at all and decided to marry me.'

'Don't be so hard on yourself. You have a lot of great qualities. And raising a child and taking care of a home is not nothing! Probably even more than what he does himself.' Mary stopped Simone and tried to defend her. She just couldn't listen to this opinion undermining women's work.

'And how is your relationship with him? Are you close? Does he treat you well?' Helen was a bit more suspicious about Marcus.

'Yes, Marcus is a good guy. He tries to help me whenever he is not busy with his work or hobbies. Sometimes he gets angry at me, but I don't think that's different to any other men. What about you, Mary? Helen?' Simone tried to shift the attention away from herself.

'I don't have children, or a husband, for that matter. Or actually, I could say that I have loads of kids, because I'm a teacher. But yeah, no family yet. I guess I'm still young and trying to enjoy myself,' Helen smiled but looked like she did not believe what she was saying.

'That's amazing, Helen. I remember you always wanted to be a teacher. And of course you are still very young and pretty, you have time. I got married too young, I don't know. But I don't regret this decision. Francis is my life, and I love my husband very much,' Simone was impressed with Helen's status and in some ways was trying to compare herself. 'What about you, Mary?' Simone asked.

'Husband and child. Standard, I guess.' Mary didn't want to talk much about it. As much as she was happy to defend other women, she actually felt that this was her weak spot. She could talk about work for hours, because she was really confident in that field.

'Ok. That's cool.' Simone was a bit disappointed with her superficial answer.

'So what is your story, Simone, I mean your mission?' Helen asked.

'Yeah, it is about infiltrating a tech company in Boston. As much as it sounds like something from a spy movie, I think it is nonsense to be honest. I don't really have time for those kinds of things. Meeting people and trying to figure out some awkward philosophical stuff,' Simone answered.

'What kind of "philosophical stuff"?' Mary asked curiously.

'Kind of to interview employees to see if they follow the same standards they are setting up for everyone using their products. I guess what it's really about is checking how hypocritical they are. Because we have no doubts that they are,' Simone laughed.

'Yeah, I would agree. I know these kinds of environments,' Mary quickly added, always wanting to offer advice or help.

'But are you going to do it?' Helen asked.

'As I said, I don't know, Helen. I have so many things on my mind.' Simone responded with an annoyed note.

'But Dad and Mum would really like you to do it. Maybe you can try your best? For them,' Helen tried to convince her.

'Hmm. We'll see.' Simone felt cornered with the argument about her parents.

'Your mission is similar, right Mary? You will be infiltrating some organisation as well, correct?' Helen asked.

'Not sure how similar. But yes, I need to get to one person in the UN. Someone powerful I guess, someone who is making some decisions that impact countries, the whole human race.' Mary sounded very excited. She loved challenging missions.

'Wow. That sounds very serious,' Simone responded.

'Yeah, maybe. But I have no idea how to start with this and whether I should start at all. The letter said something about going to Geneva … I can't really. Work, family… no time,' Mary tried to justify her unwillingness to play what in her mind were some ridiculous mind games.

'I think that's just an easy excuse, Mary!' said Helen a bit sarcastically, really wanting to challenge her. 'I remember when you were a child you always wanted to play those conspiracy games. You loved that! You watched spy movies and play-acted the roles from the movie later on. I think you should give this another thought', Helen finished, more positively.

'True. I forgot about how I loved those kinds of things when I was a child. Maybe this is the time to actually fulfil the dream of being a spy,' Mary laughed out loud. 'I just need to figure out how to get cover at work and home,' Mary added. Helen had, at least for a moment, helped her to forget about losing her parents.

'I'm pretty sure that your husband can do the job,' Simone commented, wanting to repay her for some of the questions she had received about her husband.

'My husband had a car accident some time ago. Unfortunately he is not able to move much, and won't be able to take care of our son,' Mary responded.

'Sorry to hear that,' Simone was embarrassed that she had asked.

'No worries. That's life,' Mary was not mad at her, but at the same time she hoped that this conversation would just end immediately, as she was not prepared to discuss this topic.

'Maybe I can help? I'm a bit freer these days. And my mission is pretty local so I can visit your family, probably even every day.' Helen felt happy just thinking that she might meet her sister's family.

'Will get back to you. Let me gather my thoughts about this whole "mission" thing,' Mary responded.

Mary seemed to be scared. Just yesterday, she hadn't even known what was going on with her sisters. She didn't even think about them and hadn't expected them to be there today. Now, she was close to having Helen look after her family for a few hours. This was a bit too quick for her, she always needed more time to work things out. In the meantime, the food arrived.

'This looks delicious,' Mary praised her salmon sandwich.

'And this is really tasty,' added Helen, having a bite of her wrap.

'What time is it?' Simone inquired.

It's almost 2 p.m.,' Helen said, looking at her watch.

'Oh crap. I should be going because I will miss my flight.' Simone stood up and started preparing to leave the coffee shop.

'When will we see you again, Sis?' Helen asked.

'And what about your mission?' Mary added, which sounded pretty funny considering that she also had doubts about their mission.

'I don't know. I need to think about it. Not sure if I have time for it.' Simone still sounded unconvinced.

'But that would be a good opportunity to meet up again. Don't you think? Whoever sent those letters got us together. And probably wants us to be together.' Helen was very enthusiastic about the whole situation, and she really didn't want to go back to where they had been.

'Maybe you are right.' Simone nodded.

'So will you give it a try at least? Let's keep in touch.' Helen quickly wrote her number on a piece of paper and passed it to Mary to do the same.

'Here are our phone numbers. Let's stay in touch.' Helen passed the piece of paper to Simone.

'Thank you, Helen. Let's give it a try,' responded Simone. Mary and Helen stood up and hugged Simone.

'Have a safe flight, Sis,' Mary shouted at the end.

Simone left the coffee shop. Helen and Mary sat down for another twenty minutes and finished their lunch and coffee.

'Will you give it a try, Mary?' Helen asked.

'You mean this mission?' Mary asked, to confirm.

'Yes,' Helen answered quickly.

'Hmm. Sure, why not. But I will need your help with babysitting.' Mary had already thought this thing through. This was a great opportunity to rebuild a relationship with her sister.

'Of course. Always.' Helen sounded excited and happy.

'Let's stay in touch,' said Mary, and exchanged phone numbers with Helen.

'Great. Let me pay the bill.' Helen stood up and went to the counter to pay for lunch. It was very uncommon for coffee shops in those days to have no electronic payment option on the app, or at the table. This was an old-school place where conversation between people, even across the counter, was really important. She came back to the table, hugged Mary goodbye and they both left the coffee shop.

***

On their way home, each of the four sisters thought about what a day it had been. So many things to think about. Their past, today, and their future. There was something very exciting in all of that and they all felt this – even if they didn't admit it, like Constance.

Helen was the most excited of all. Loneliness was killing her. She missed her sisters a lot. Now they were back together. Hopefully for a longer time this time. 'This was a good day,' Helen said to herself, smiling as she laid down on her bed at home.

Sometime later, Helen's phone started ringing and vibrating. She woke up and grabbed the phone, and sleepily asked, 'Hello, how can I help you'?

'Hey Helen, sorry for ringing you. Constance here. You sound like you were asleep.'

'Hey Conny, how are you doing? Yes, It seems I fell asleep when I got home. Is everything alright?' Helen asked, more awake now that she knew it was Constance.

'Yeah, all good … but I was thinking about your offer of a place to crash, is that still available?' Constance asked with no confidence, thinking that Helen had just been trying to be polite.

'Of course, Sis! You are more than welcome to come over here and sleep at my place, I have a spare bed. We'll be fine,' Helen replied, smiling to herself.

'That's great. I'm gonna be there in three minutes,' shouted Conny and hung up.

'Wow, three minutes. She must be across the road.' Helen went to the window and looked out. 'Yep, there she is, my little sister.' Helen smiled again.

Constance came up to the third floor of Helen's apartment building. Helen opened the door and Constance hugged her very firmly.

'Good to see you, Conny,' Helen grinned at her.

'Thank you for having me, Helen. I really appreciate it.' Constance was thankful.

'Sure, always. Are you hungry? Have you had anything to eat? Helen asked.

'Since breakfast … not really,' Conny responded quickly.

'What? Since breakfast? You must be starving. Let's get some pizza, I know a great pizza place just close to the park.' Helen quickly asked the assistant to order pizza. In the meantime Constance started walking around her place.

'Cosy. Is it yours or are you renting?' Conny asked and grabbed some strawberries that were on the counter.

'You know how much an apartment costs in Manhattan? I can barely afford the rent. I see you are still into strawberries. Clean them first, not sure how long they've been there,' Helen smiled, looking at Conny picking up some strawberries.

'Yeah, don't worry. A bit of dust on strawberries won't kill me. These taste decent,' said Constance, her mouth full of strawberries.

Tap, tap, tap! Something tapped at Helen's window.

'And here is our pizza,' Helen exclaimed.

'What? How?' Conny seemed surprised.

'Really, Sis? You have never seen pizza delivery by drone? What year are you living in? Helen opened the window and collected the pizza box.

'Incredible. Yeah, I probably still live in the 2020s.'

'Let's grab something to drink and sit on the couch,' Helen suggested and they both sat down.

'I guess TV is also something that got left behind in the 2020s,' Conny laughed.

'No. There are other entertainment devices you can use now. Not sure if those are TVs. More online streaming stuff. But I prefer silence anyway. Maybe I'm just weird.'

'Silence? I hate silence,' responded Conny and started eating the pizza.

'So what happened after our parents died? I remember you went to Aunt Vivian. I sent some letters to you but I never got any response. I guess the government wanted us to be separated, so I imagine they interfered with any communication between us,' Helen said.

'Yes, good old Aunt Vivian. She didn't have an easy life with me. I would say that it didn't have to be the government interfering with our communication, I'm pretty sure I didn't do much to gain Auntie's trust or even willingness to be nice to me, so you know …' Conny had another bite of pizza.

'What did you do to her?' Helen asked

'Not much, I think, but that in a sense could be bad as well. I ran away from home a few times. Didn't really pay too much attention at school. I dropped out of school a few times. Didn't talk much to Auntie either, so I was just this troubled kid in her eyes.' Constance responded.

'Nice. I'm sure you added some grey hair to Auntie's head. What happened after school? You are 20 now, right?'

'Yes. When I graduated, I kind of escaped again and I don't think Auntie bothered to search for me again. I was 18 at the time.'

'Wow. That's like out of a movie. So, what have you been doing for the last two years? What have you been up to? Where have you been living?' Helen bombarded Conny with more questions, she was so keen to know more about her not-so-little-anymore sister.

'That's quite a few questions you have for me,' Conny smiled.

'I'm sorry, it's just that I haven't seen you for so long. And I just missed you a lot, like your sisters.' Helen felt like she might start to cry in a minute.

'Don't worry. I get it,' Conny hugged her. 'So, life was not too easy on me. Maybe I won't go into too many details, but I slept basically wherever, met some friends on the streets of New York … yeah, maybe friends is too big of a word. Some guys maybe would be more accurate.' Constance reflected on this for a second.

'Oh, I didn't expect this. So how have you been getting money? Food?' Helen was digging more.

'Yeah, about that …' Constance faltered.

'Too soon. Let's maybe not get into so many details. Have some more pizza, Sis.' Helen stopped herself.

'Sure. This is actually great pizza, I must admit.' Conny had another bite.

'So have you thought more about your mission Conny? Are you going for it or not?' Helen changed the topic after a moment of silence.

'I guess so. I have nothing else to do so I might just try. Still, it seems a bit silly to me. But there is some money for expenses, so … nothing to lose. Of course it would just be easier to spend that money and skip the whole mission thing … but maybe I haven't sunk that low yet and want to be at least a bit honest about it. But I'm not sure about those organisations, what they do and what they are up to. Not sure how I can make peace between them,' Constance said.

'Let's look them up,' Helen responded

'Sure, let me get the letter with their names,' Conny got up and got the letter from her jacket.

'Here you go,' she passed the letter to Helen and pointed out the names. Helen took out her mobile device and entered the names into the browser.

'Ok. It is clear now. One of the organisations is a pro-life organisation and the second one is a pro-choice organisation. Interesting,' Helen said and looked at Conny.

'Hmm. Okay. I don't think I know where to start with this. I'm not very into social issues like this. I've never really thought about this problem. I guess it won't be easy to find common ground,' Conny looked a bit scared of her mission now.

'Yeah, that's a difficult one. What do you know about this topic at all? Let's maybe start with that,' Helen said

'So on one side we have folks who just want to allow women to decide when they want to be mothers. Not everyone is ready, or some circumstances can make you want to delay this thing.

I guess in most countries this is how it is now,' Conny said.

'Yeah, I'm looking at their website and they say that there are only a few countries where they have to fight for a woman's full right to decide about her body. Poland, Switzerland,' said Helen, looking at the screen.

'Oh. Ok. That makes sense. Poland? Is that not where Mum was from?' Conny asked.

'Yeah. I knew some Polish words that Mum taught me when I was little,' Helen reflected on this and tried to remember them.

'Hmm. I don't really remember much to be honest. Mum and Dad weren't at home much at some points in my childhood …'

'What about the second organisation?' Helen put an end to this sad moment.

'I guess they don't want women to decide about their lives and bodies. Sounds like archaic Christian madness,' Conny laughed.

'I don't think it is so simple, but it definitely sounds like an idea that's not of this world we are living in.' Helen smiled and started searching for some more information about this organisation.

'Hmm. Weird. It seems like their websites are blocked. Cannot open them here. Why is that?' Helen wondered.

'Interesting. Show it to me, my first boyfriend was a hacker who always wanted to fight with the establishment. He showed me a few tricks.' Helen handed over her device to Constance.

'Let me quickly look at the settings. You don't mind if I quickly download a different browser for you?' Conny asked, but didn't wait for an answer – she had just done it. After a minute of working on Helen's phone, Conny tried to open the web pages again.

'Here you go.' Conny gave the cell phone back to Helen and smiled.

'Thanks. Cool. I hope I don't have the FBI knocking on my door tomorrow,' Helen winked at Conny.

'No. You shouldn't have. Usually it takes them a few days longer to figure out those things, and you have to do something illegal.' Conny responded quickly and seriously.

'How do you know all of those things?' Helen seemed to be surprised at the knowledge Conny had.

'They told me once,' Conny responded without hesitating.

'What? How come? The FBI visited you? When?' Helen seemed even more surprised.

'Yeah … Long story. My boyfriend … and, you know …' Conny paused. 'So what about this organisation? What's on the website?' she changed the topic, trying not to share too many embarrassing moments from her life.

'Human life is holy. Given to us by our Creator. We have no right to end any human life. Helen started reading from their website.

'How the heck will I find common ground for those two groups? They sound like they have nothing in common.' Conny scratched her head.

'Hmm. It won't be easy. But you have to meet with them!' Helen exclaimed.

'Yeah, sure. I don't mind flying to Switzerland. Just need to check if my documents and passport are still valid. And what do you think about all of this stuff? I remember you were this girl who was more sensitive about morality, and people, in general.' Conny wondered.

'This is a difficult one. I believe in God, I think. Or at least that we are not alone in this universe. Not sure how strong that is, but still something I have left from our parents, some kind of seed of belief they planted in me, that we are not alone here. It is not easy to believe these days. Not many opportunities. At the same time, I think that it is necessary to have hope that this life is not everything. Considering all the sadness, problems and evil in this world, without this hope it is pretty much impossible to live. Abortion is a very sensitive issue. In some ways I understand that life is sacred, and we should care about those who cannot defend themselves. But I understand the situation when a woman can find herself in such a difficult position that she cannot see any other option. That's probably our fault, all of ours, because we are not supporting those women at all, so we limit their options. And in some ways it is easy to blame them for killing a child. But is it not the case that we make them kill their children? Maybe not directly, but us not doing much to support them or their children, kind of puts some responsibility on us all, on society.'

'That's very interesting. I guess I need to study this topic a bit more before I start the discussion with them. Thank you Helen!' Conny hugged Helen again.

'I remembered that you were a hugger but didn't realise that it was so strong in you,' Helen laughed. 'Ok. It is getting late now. We should go to sleep.'

'Good idea,' Conny agreed.

'The bathroom is just there,' Helen pointed out a black door that was closed.

'Thanks!' Conny responded and ran to the bathroom, where she spent a few minutes. In the meantime, Helen prepared a bed for her and lay down on the couch beside it.

'There was no need for this. I could sleep wherever,' Conny said when Helen showed her to the bed.

'No problem at all. You are my guest, you are my sister. You can't sleep on the couch,' Helen was very insistent.

'I could. This is much more than I've had in the last two years, so ...'

'No more discussion. Let's get some sleep,' Helen replied and went to the bathroom quickly. When she came back she found that Constance was almost asleep.

'Goodnight, little Sis.' Helen kissed Conny's forehead

'Goodnight and thank you for everything,' Conny responded with a sleepy voice. Helen lay down on the couch and was very candid in her response. Helen was a bit like a mother to Conny, and Conny felt this unconditional love from Helen.

'I'm so happy that you are here. I missed you so much. You are probably asleep now but please feel free to stay here as long as you want ...'   she paused for a minute, waiting for a response. 'Sleep well, Sis,' said Helen, thinking that Conny was asleep.

'You don't even know how lonely I am sometimes …' Helen finished the sentence quietly and closed her eyes. Conny opened her eyes, and a tear ran down her chin. 'Poor Helen. I missed her so much …' she thought and closed her eyes again.

4

Helen started a group text chat.

Helen
Morning ladies. I can't believe it is already a week since we met in person again! I'm so glad that we found the courage to go over to our old house. How was your week? Have you moved forward with your 'missions' at all? I'm starting a new job at the school this coming Monday! Exciting times!

Conny
Not bad at all, thanks for asking Helen

Mary
Hey Helen, did some research with Conny on people involved in our missions.

Conny
And we are going to Geneva tomorrow!

Mary
Yeah, exactly. There are some potential opportunities for us this week to meet those people, so we decided to fly over.

Helen
Do you need any help with taking care of your husband and child, Mary?

Mary
No, we should be good. Eugene's sister will be able
to cover for me this week. Thanks Helen.

Helen
Wondering how Simone is doing … hey, Simone?
How are things with you?

Simone
Apologies girls. A bit of stuff going on today. Yeah, all
fine here. I figured out how I can get closer to this
tech company. I will pretend to be a journalist! Haha
… Already got some info on who I should contact,
etc. Should be fine.

Helen
Nice one! Way to go, Sis! So it seems all the good
fun will start this week. Let me know if I can be of any
help to you all?!

Conny
Will do. Cheers, Helen Mary – what time do we meet
tomorrow? Which airport?

Mary
JFK. Flight is at 5 p.m. so I suggest meeting there
around 2.30 p.m.?

Conny
Sounds good.

Helen.
Constance, do you have your ID ready?

Conny
Yeah, it was actually pretty easy to get it. They have those bio-AI whatever passports now. Pretty clever stuff to be frank.

Helen
Good stuff. I have no clue what you use these days to travel internationally, I don't remember the last time I was abroad.

Simone
When all of this is finished, we should go for a vacation somewhere! Together!

Mary
Great call Simone! I'm up for that. There is still a lot to catch up on. Would be great if our families could meet each other as well.

Conny.
+1

Helen
Sounds like a plan! Have a safe trip to Switzerland!

Hey Mary! How's it going? You here long?
Constance came up to Mary, at Gate 21 in Terminal
5 at JFK airport and hugged her.

'Conny, good to see you again. My little sister.'
Mary smiled.

'Not so little anymore,' Constance responded with a
smile. 'Do you want to grab some lunch or coffee?'
she asked.

'I'm full, so no food. Got something to eat before I
left the house. But sure, I'll grab a coffee. I've been
up since 5 a.m. this morning.'

'Since 5 a.m.? Wow …that's a bit early. Let's head
to the coffee shop just over there, around the corner,'
Conny pointed in the direction of a coffee shop.

'Why were you up so early?' she asked Mary.

'I had to prepare everything before my trip. I had a
tough week in the office, so had no time to sort out a
few things,' Mary answered.

'By the way, thanks for checking a few things for
me about those organisations. It is very hard to hack
anywhere from Helen's devices. And she freaks out
every time I try to do something like that. I guess the
story about the FBI scared her or something,'
Constance laughed.

'FBI? Sounds like we have more to catch up on on
the plane!' They got to the coffee shop and ordered
coffees and a sandwich.

'Yeah, it was pretty difficult to find those folks
online. It seems that they are not so popular with
those who run the internet these days …' Mary
continued.

'I know, kind of weird. I realised that when I was doing the first search with Helen. It seems like whatever they are doing it is not really legal everywhere. Their sites were blocked.' Conny seemed to be surprised by this.

'Conny and Mary, coffees and a sandwich!' the girl shouted from over the counter.

'That's us!' Conny got up quickly and picked up coffees and the sandwich for herself.

'This looks nice,' Conny said to herself and took a first bite.

'So what's the story with your husband? Is he sick or something? I saw your message about caring for him,' Constance mumbled with her mouth full of sandwich.

'Not sure exactly what you said … but I guess you are talking about Eugene. He had a car accident a few years back. He can't walk, he is in a wheelchair.'

'Oh, wow. That's tough, I guess. How do you cope with that?' Conny asked.

'I think I'm just used to it now. But it's not easy sometimes. Definitely when we need to make some decisions about our son's life and yeah … that can be a bit challenging,' Mary responded.

'Sorry for digging more, but how? What do you mean?' Constance insisted. As much as she was interested in the topic, mostly she was just happy to be spending some time with her oldest sister. Mary had left home when Conny was just 11 and she hadn't seen her for a long time. Had never had a real conversation with her, either. Mary, at the time, had been a typical teenager who was not interested in babysitting her younger siblings. Now, finally, they were having a conversation as two equals.

'He is fully paralysed. He can't move at all. Or speak. We have some equipment that reads his brain waves to understand what he thinks. Mostly it is just trying to figure out 'yes' or 'no' answers. But I trust my gut a bit. And I look into his eyes to get the answer.' Mary was pretty relaxed talking about this.

'That's amazing in some ways. I'm surprised that they haven't figured out yet how to fix those kinds of problems.' Conny was astonished by Mary's response.

'They kind of have, but I think it is not there yet in the sense of accuracy and possibilities. I think the human brain is incredibly complex and full of secrets that cannot be fully figured out by a computer/AI system.' Mary answered.

'You were saying that this happened because of a car crash? I thought with all of these self-driving cars there were no car accidents.' Conny tried to get more information from Mary.

'But some people still like to drive their cars themselves. I'm still driving my car!' Mary exclaimed.

'I never had a car, never learned to drive, so I don't really know the feeling, but I believe that some people just love it,' Conny smiled, happy that the conversation had moved this way.

'We should get going so we don't miss our flight.' Mary got up and started walking.

The flight to Geneva was full. Mostly businesspeople, or UN administration. Luckily enough there was not much turbulence, as usually happened these days. Global warming had really affected the comfort of travelling. At least this was what scientists were saying. As we know, many years later it was discovered that all of this investing in saving the earth didn't do much good. There was no real threat, at least in the short-term. Obviously human beings were always working towards destroying nature and the earth. But not all the data presented by enlightened scientists actually made sense. Some people got very rich because of this and that was probably the only good thing to come out of all of that, at least for them. There were many cancelled and delayed flights every day around the globe. Humanity started to look at different modes of transport so as not to be as affected by the weather. But for long-haul journeys, flying was still the quickest way to get to your final destination.

***

'Hi, my name is Jenny Moskovitz and I'm a freelance blogger writing about the IT industry. I would like to meet with Mr Greg O'Donnell.' Simone was practising in front of the mirror in her room. She put on some glasses, changed her hairstyle and put on more hipster clothes. 'I think that was pretty good, let's do it,' she said to herself.

'The headquarters of this tech company were only thirty minutes from her house. Traffic wasn't bad that morning, probably because she left the house after rush hour. She got there even quicker than the thirty minutes estimated by her app. It was a fancy and shiny building that was pretty easy to spot on the grey and dark street. Automatic glass doors welcomed her – literally welcomed her, by saying, 'Welcome to Lievy'. 'That's very kind,' she thought. She walked up to the reception desk and said: 'Hi, My name is Jenny Moskovitz and I'm a freelance blogger writing about the IT industry. I would like to meet with Mr Greg O'Donnell.'

'Hi, do you have an appointment?' the receptionist responded very quickly.

'Hmm. So I'm done now,' Simone thought. 'No, not really,' she responded, losing all hope.

'Let me check with Mr O'Donnell,' the receptionist smiled and started typing something on her keyboard.

'Miss Moskovitz, please take a seat. Mr O'Donnell will be available in ten minutes.'

'Thank you,' Simone smiled and sat down. 'That was lucky,' she said quietly to herself. Ten minutes went by very quickly. Simone was looking around the reception, which was full of interesting gadgets. 'I should probably take some notes, or record something here, like professional journalists do,' she thought to herself. 'What am I doing here?' She was really surprised that she had actually done it. She thought this was just silly, to pretend to be someone else, she didn't really have time for something like this, and realistically she wasn't qualified in any of the fields here. She was neither a journalist nor an IT person. The only thing that really kept her going was the fact that she could share something with her sisters again, and this gave her the sense of purpose that she was unconsciously looking for.

'Mr O'Donnell is coming down now,' the receptionist announced.

'Thank you,' responded Simone and got up. A minute later, a handsome 45-year-old man in a polo shirt and jeans came through a pink automatic door. 'Bye Greg,' the doors responded to him walking through.

'Miss Moskovitz, it is a pleasure meeting you. I'm a huge fan of your blog,' the man said to Simone without hesitating.

'You are? That's awesome, I guess,' Simone responded, not really knowing what he was talking about. She thought he must have mistaken her for someone else

'Let's go to the coffee shop on the second floor,' Greg said and let her go ahead of him through the door.

'Thank you,' Simone responded, but was interrupted by the door assistant welcoming Greg back. Hearing that again unexpectedly gave Simone a fright.

'Sorry about that, we don't really notice this voice anymore but I understand that it is something new for other people,' Greg looked at her and smiled. They used the stairs to get to the second floor.

'We believe that it is important these days to challenge yourself physically and use the stairs more often. This is why we don't have elevators in our building,' Greg explained.

'I guess that makes sense, considering all of the automation and robotics in many industries and in our lives, we don't really use our muscles so often anymore,' Simone responded on the spot.

'Exactly. Our employees' wellbeing is very important to us. And we know how simple physical exercise, like taking the stairs, can improve their wellbeing, and just make them happier in the long term,' Greg responded proudly. They got to some doors that did not really look like doors. They kind of felt like they were a wardrobe door to an old-school Narnia world. But then on the other side it was just a fancy coffee shop. They sat down at the glass table, which was a wireless charger, as Simone noticed a second after she put her mobile device on the table.

'Wow. That's cool,' she said.

'Yeah, it is a pretty old product. But we still need to charge our batteries somehow.'

'Greg and Simone! Coffee's ready!' the voice at the counter announced.

'Simone?' Greg asked.

'Yeah, that's my real name. J. Moskovitz is just my professional name,' Simone tried to turn that around quickly.

'How come this thing knew what I drink?' she changed the topic quickly.

'You pay with your phone when you buy a coffee in coffee shops, so there are records of what coffees you order.' Greg got up to pick up the coffees.

'Oh wow, that's a bit unexpected, the transparency of my coffee preferences,' Simone added quietly. For a second she paused and thought about other things that this smart building might know about her already.

She felt very insecure. 'I'm glad I have no real secrets,' she thought to herself.

'But this should not be a surprise for you, right?' Greg returned to the table. You wrote about that in one of your blog posts, "Automated coffee: New meanings?"'.

'Oh yeah,' Simone nodded.

'Unfortunately, I don't have much time, so can we start this interview?' Greg asked politely.

'Of course,' Simone nodded and took out her notepad.

'Wow, I did not expect this from the world-class IT blogger … an old-school paper notepad,' Greg laughed out loud.

'It is made from recycled paper, so no trees were hurt … at least in recent years. Let's start then!' It was getting too awkward for Simone.

'How seriously is Lievy taking women's influence in the world of technology?' Simone asked.

'Without a doubt, Lievy is very serious about gender equality, and about ensuring that our senior leadership team is properly balanced, which means that we hope that women have the same influence in the world of technology as men,' Greg gave a very quick and straight answer.

'Could you please give me some examples of women in Lievy who have had a huge impact on the industry?' Simone was trying to dig more.

'Of course. Jo Kavanagh's patents have impacted the whole industry in various ways. They have changed the way people think about online payments.' Greg was proud that he was able to answer that question quickly.

'The same Jo Kavanagh who said in an interview last week that she was harassed by men in this company and could not stand it anymore and left?' Simone felt a bit happy that he had mentioned her, because just last week she had read an article about her on the plane.

'I haven't read the article, so I can't comment,' Greg tried to be as politically correct as possible.

'But is she still working at the company?' Simone asked.

'No. She resigned recently for personal reasons … Maybe I used the wrong example. There are many more talented female engineers in our company who have impacted the industry with their ideas. For example Janet …' Greg wasn't able to finish the sentence.

'No no. Let's go back to Jo. What policies do you have internally to ensure women are treated equally and are not harassed by powerful men?' Simone did not want to give up on this topic.

'We have many policies around this. We try to react as quickly as possible when those things happen,' Greg answered.

'How often do "those things" happen?' Simone felt more confident.

'Not very often. Rarely, I would say,' Greg said and started looking at his phone.

'That's not a very accurate response for a technology company that is "data driven". Do you have any reports?' Simone pushed harder. She was feeling the 'flow', and had forgotten about the discomfort she had felt ten minutes earlier. She smelled blood like a hungry shark. She felt he was definitely hiding something.

'Apologies, but I will have to go now. Just got a ping that something has come up and I need to be at a meeting.' Greg stood up and simply left. Obviously it was a lie, but Greg didn't feel like finishing this interview. There were no more topics he felt confident bringing up.

'Ok …' Simone was kind of surprised. 'I will find my own way out,' she threw in at the end.

'Yeah, yeah … it's easy to find your way out of here,' Greg said to her over his shoulder. Simone left the building. She didn't really know what to think about that conversation. Maybe she was just too pushy and this guy just could not take that anymore. Maybe he felt offended or insulted. She thought to herself about all the questions she had still wanted to ask while looking at her notepad.

The next day, Simone went for a walk in the evening. She passed the Lievy buildings and found herself thinking about what to do next. 'Do I even understand what those technology companies are doing?' she asked herself. 'What about gender equality? I guess there was a bit more to discover,' she thought.

Suddenly she saw Greg. The same guy, from yesterday. She wondered if she should talk to him once again. He wasn't alone. He was with a woman. They were a similar age and were holding hands. Simone had a quick look at her phone. 'Yep, it has to

be his wife,' she whispered to herself. They were
arguing, pretty loudly. They were not sober, for sure.
It seemed like they were not leaving the Lievy offices
but the local bar, which was almost next door to their
office. She didn't know why, but she decided to follow
them. 'Who knows, maybe they will lead me to
something,' she thought, like an experienced old
detective who always sees something suspicious
even if it's only in his vivid imagination.

After three blocks, they turned right and went into a
Chinese restaurant. Simone followed them, but she
wasn't very hungry. She sat pretty close to them. The
restaurant wasn't busy at all. There was barely
anyone there besides the three of them. Greg looked
at Simone, but turned away again quickly. Simone
didn't look like she had the day before when she was
in his office. Maybe when he heard her voice he
would recognise her, but Simone tried to speak as
quietly as possible when talking to the waiter. Greg
and his wife were not quiet. They were still arguing,
and it seemed they were both losing patience.
Simone had thought that Greg was only lying when
talking about gender equality and now everyone
could see how he was treating his own wife. This was
her chance. Greg was drunk. And we all know how
honest people can be after drinking alcohol. They
can reveal the biggest secrets about themselves and
others. Suddenly the woman stood up and shouted: 'I
can't take your shit anymore, this relationship is a
joke!' and she left to go to the restroom.
Simone stood up and followed her. When she got to
the restroom, she saw Greg's wife crying. She was

trying to hide it, and ensure her makeup was not ruined.

'Is everything all right?' Simone asked.

'Yes. Why are you asking?' the woman responded quickly and firmly.

'I saw you arguing with your partner, and now you're crying,' Simone replied empathetically.

'Could you please mind your own business?' the woman could not control her anger.

'Listen,' Simone came closer, 'I'm a woman as well. Men are jerks. I know what you are feeling right now.' Simone was making this up as she went along. Funnily enough she didn't feel the same way towards Marcus.

'Do you?' The woman didn't want to believe some random girl in the restaurant bathroom.

'Of course. I have cried over men often. What did this jerk do to you? Did he cheat?' Simone was trying to get some more info about the 'real' Greg.

'No. Or maybe, I don't know. But he is just such a hypocrite. He has no respect for women at all. He is treating me like shit. He thinks that I'm his servant. He is giving me rewards and punishments like to a little kid. He treats women at work better, because he has to. He is a VP, he needs to care about the culture of respect, diversity and gender equality. But when he gets home, he is just a pig.' That was much easier to get from her than Simone had thought. Everything had been served to her on a plate here. She felt guiltily happy that she had actually come into the restaurant and followed this woman.

'Hmm. I'm sorry to hear that. Do you want to go somewhere else and get a few drinks? By the way, I'm Simone, What's your name?'

'I'm Claire. Nice to meet you. Yeah, sure. I don't want to see this jerk anymore.' Claire and Simone left the toilet and the restaurant. Claire didn't even say goodbye to her husband. 'He can wait, I don't care!' she said to Simone. They went to the nearest bar and chatted for another few hours. Simone felt great, not because of Claire's sadness and this weird situation, but because of her mission. She had finally found what she was looking for and she had this feeling that she could be useful and help her. She started to understand Claire's issues very well. She felt empathy for her. She felt very close to her. Claire mentioned that her husband was working on some gender-related project called GD1. Simone decided to do more research. 'I might be getting somewhere with my mission here,' she thought to herself as she was walking home.

Helen left the school premises just after lunchtime. The way home wasn't as nice as from her previous school but still, when the weather was nice it didn't matter. A sunny day in New York is always great, it doesn't matter which park you walk through.

'So far, so good,' she thought to herself when thinking back over her first days at the new job. Then her phone started beeping. She took it out of her pocket and had a look at the screen.

It was a text message, which she hadn't seen in ages. The message was from Mary:

Hey Sis, hope I didn't freak you out with this text message, but for some reason the internet doesn't work on my cell. Listen, would you be able to come over to my apartment to look after Eugene and John on Saturday? Eugene's sister will have to leave earlier on Saturday, and I won't come back until 10 p.m.

Helen replied quickly without even thinking about it that of course she could come over. She was excited. She really wanted to know more about her sisters. She wanted to know their families and friends. Just to be a part of their lives again. She couldn't fall asleep that night. She was thinking about what John and Eugene would look like and how they would react when they saw her. She was not afraid of John. Kids are kids. You have to expect the unexpected. She was always good with minding and talking to kids, so she was not scared at all. With Eugene though she had some doubts. That would be a new experience for her. Obviously she wanted to make a good impression and she wanted him to like her. The question was how to make it happen. She finally fell asleep around 3 a.m., so she had a hard time getting up the next morning. She woke up at 8.30 a.m. 'Oh shit, I'll be late!' she shouted. She got up quickly, took a quick shower and ran to school. She was late, but no one really seemed to care. It took some time for kids to actually get to class, so no one really noticed that Helen was late. 'It would be terrible to be late in the first week and have to have a chat with the school principal…' she thought to herself.

The day went well until the last class. The girls in that class were pretty mature. They were very confident and they didn't seem to understand the difference between their role and their teacher's role. That was pretty common in those days. Everyone felt like they were qualified to have an opinion on every topic. But at the end of the day that was just an opinion without any knowledge whatsoever. It was the last class of the day. Everyone was tired and their thoughts were already on weekend parties and entertainment.

'Miss, as you are new here … there is a rule in this school …'one girl started.

'Yes?' Helen asked.

'Yeah, the rule is that new teachers need to answer one question. We are very transparent here and we don't want teachers here to be hiding their secrets …' the blonde girl continued. That sounded very odd to Helen, but at the same time she really wanted to gain their trust, so she went for it.

'Ok. I'm not a serial killer, if that's what you are asking,' Helen laughed.

'That's great, but I have a different question,' the girl quickly answered.

'Sure. I will answer,' Helen played the confident woman.

'We did some research about you,' a friend of the blonde girl added.

'You did, really. Okay,' Helen replied, starting to lose ground.

'Yes. So we wanted to know something about your relationships with men. Are you still a virgin? Have you had a sex with men at all? We know that you are not dating anyone now, and you haven't for quite a long time.' The blonde girl had no difficulty asking these questions. The other girls just giggled.

'Ah, yeah …' Helen was surprised by this very personal question. This was not an easy topic for her.

'That is really a personal question. I don't know if I want to answer it,' Helen responded, like she had been given a choice.

'We are trying to be transparent in this school. And you said you would answer any question,' the blonde girl's best friend responded.

'Sure, but I'm not confident that this is an appropriate conversation or topic of conversation … my sex life.' Helen felt embarrassed. All of these teenage girls were looking at her. Waiting for her answer. That felt very weird. On the one hand, Helen knew that these kinds of topics were not taboo anymore. But on the other hand these girls' approach, intimidating her, was just wrong as well.

'Do you have anything to hide?' the blonde girl added. That really hurt Helen. Not everyone needs to be an exhibitionist. It was her right to not say everything. People's lives today were just constantly examined like through an X-ray machine. Every little piece. You had to be really good at hiding if you wanted to escape from this scrutiny. And she was hiding something. Her personal history, which was not easy. She just did not want to share her private business with the whole world.

'I think this class is over now. Have a great weekend.' Helen tried to save herself by dismissing the class. The girls left the class quickly. Helen sat down on her chair and looked out the window, thinking about what she should do. In one way she didn't want to answer this question, and she was lucky that this question had only been asked just now. She could prepare to answer it, if she decided to do so at all. On the other hand, she knew that she should do it as she was trying to build a relationship with these girls, build trust between them. Without honesty it wouldn't happen and she would fail in her mission. Helen stood up, took her bag and left the class.

'Miss Murphy, do you have a sec?' the blonde girl who had asked the question in class was waiting for Helen outside.

'Of course, I hope you don't have more personal questions,' Helen tried to play it cool.

'About that. I'm sorry for the question. But I'm in a situation where my boyfriend is putting some pressure on me, and he wants us to start having sex and I don't know what to do …' the blonde girl didn't seem to be so confident anymore.

'Oh. Don't be sorry, Jane.' Helen hugged her. Have you talked to your mum?' Helen asked.

'Not really. We don't really have a relationship. She is constantly busy with her work. Dad is the same. I would probably not speak to Dad about that, anyway, he might freak out or something. Probably speaking

to either of them would not be such a great idea.'
Jane was now feeling shy and could not look into
Helen's eyes.

'I understand. Why then are you coming to me? I'm
new at this school.' Helen seemed very surprised.

'Yeah, but there is something about you that tells
me that you can help me here,' Jane answered.

'Ok. So I will probably have to think about it a bit
more, but for now I can say: Don't rush into anything.
You don't want to regret anything.'

'That's why you didn't answer my question in class,
because you regret your decision?' Jane pushed.

'No. Maybe. I think I should go.' Helen was
confused. She didn't know how to handle the
situation.

'Ok. Have a great weekend Miss Murphy,' Jane
smiled and went to her car.

'Bye,' Helen replied. 'Wow. That's quite the ending
for my first week at this new school,' Helen thought.
Helen went home and got something to eat on the
way. She was still thinking about how to answer this
question. It was not just a matter of whether she
answered a group of curious girls. She wanted to
help Jane, and not giving an answer might be bad for
her.

Helen didn't sleep well. She was practising in her
head how she should answer Jane's question. She
was also stressed about meeting Mary's husband
and son. She woke up pretty early, around 7 a.m.
She got some breakfast and orange juice. 'I guess it
is time to go,' she thought to herself. She packed her
bag and went to get a car.

Traffic was ok, so she got to Mary's apartment quickly. She rang the bell and someone let her in. She went upstairs and found the door was already open. She entered.

'Hi. Anybody here?' Helen asked.

'Hey Helen. I'm Jo. Gotta go. Thank you for staying with them,' a brown-haired girl in a red shirt and black skirt quickly closed the door and disappeared.

'Oh, well ….bye,' Helen responded quietly.

'Hello, who are you?' A little boy came up to Helen with some snacks in his hand.

'I'm Helen, your mum's sister. I'm your aunt.' Helen smiled and shook his hand.

'Ok "Auntie". How come I have never heard about you?' The boy was curious.

'Yeah. That's probably something you should ask your mum when she comes back.' It was much easier for Helen to speak to a little boy, than to teenage girl about sex.

'Ok,' the boy replied with a smile and ran away.

'That was easy,' Helen thought happily. She moved to another room. Eugene, Mary's husband, was sitting in a wheelchair and looking out the window.

'Hello,' Helen said. There was no response. It was quiet. Helen walked up to Eugene's wheelchair and showed herself to him. He looked at her wordlessly.

'Hello, my name is Helen. I'm Mary's sister. Nice to meet you,' Helen introduced herself. There was no reaction. Helen remembered that Mary had said that he had some way of communicating. As much as Helen wanted to get to know Eugene and John better, John was not too chatty, and unfortunately Eugene could not speak.

Eugene's sister had left a note saying what and when they needed to eat and that was pretty much all she had learned about the two most important people in her sister's life. But she tried to observe their behaviour. She was curious how much of her sister she would see in John. She didn't know at the time that John had been adopted because Mary and Eugene couldn't have children. No one really describes their child as adopted in the first conversation. Even if a child is adopted you should always be able to see the parents' love in the child.

She looked at John. 'Definitely, he looks like Mary.' His eyes and smiles were almost the same. He was really focused as well, whatever he was doing he was 100% focused on the job. She looked at Eugene as well. She had never cared for a disabled person, so it was a challenge for her, at least at the start. She thought that there was something beautiful in not being capable of helping yourself. Living in a limited world. Dependent on others. And it was not like wishing for this kind of life, but being an adult and at the same time being a child who cannot do anything for himself leaves a lot of space for love, goodness and God.

This was not a common situation anymore. There were almost no people with Down syndrome. In many countries disabled people were treated as useless who did not bring any benefits to society. As terrible as it sounds, that was unfortunately the reality in 2037.

Women had problems getting pregnant and giving birth much more often. Even in vitro fertilisation did not work as well as people thought. There were also some people who followed the trend and decided to have no children at all just to save resources on earth for future generations. So kind.

The time seemed to pass very slowly, but it was not long before Mary arrived.

'Hey, Sis. thank you very much for your help today!' she shouted as she came in the door.

'No worries, Sis. It was a pleasure. Great meeting your family!' Helen responded. 'Where is Conny?'

'She went home already. It was a hard week for her.' Mary went to another room to give a kiss to John and Eugene.

'Oh … you poor little thing.' Mary said, standing beside Eugene's wheelchair.

'Yeah, I thought you said that he has a way of communicating?' Helen asked.

'He does, but it seems that the transmitter has switched itself off. Let me turn it back on,' Mary said and switched the transmitter back on.

'Thank you …' Eugene's simulated voice said through the transmitter.

'I guess that's for you, Helen,' Mary said, winking at her.

'So, how was Geneva?' Helen asked.

'There is a lot to tell. Come to my place tomorrow, we will have breakfast. Bring Conny with you. It was a long day.'

'Sure thing, get some rest, Sis.' Helen hugged her.

'Thank you so much, again. You saved my life,' Mary gave Helen a kiss on the cheek.

'Of course,' Helen responded and quickly left the apartment. She felt great. They were one family again. She was there for her sisters. And she believed that her sisters would help her, as well. Mary had similar thoughts. Looking at the happy faces of Eugene and John she found herself thinking, 'Why did I not reach out to them earlier?'

***

On Sunday the four sisters all had breakfast at Mary's. 'So, how was your trip, girls?' Helen asked.

'Fruitful, I would say.' Mary responded. 'Conny, do you want to start? I will make some coffee.' Mary got up and went to the coffee machine.

'Yes, it was an interesting experience, but I'm very tired now. I fell asleep very quickly yesterday, that's why I didn't even hear you come home, Helen' Constance stated.

'Yeah, I guessed that you were tired when I almost tripped over your bags behind the front door.' Helen smiled.

'Sorry about that, sister, I literally fell into bed seconds after I got into the apartment,' Conny tried to explain herself.

'No worries Conny, how did your mission go?' Helen asked.

'Yeah! I'm still trying to get my head around that. It's not easy. I met the leaders of those two groups. They have very radical views, in contradiction with each other. It is so extremely difficult to find common ground for them both. But everything comes from their experience, really. Their views are pretty much determined by what they have experienced. One is a survivor of abortion of some kind. He was meant not to live or was not expected to have the greatest quality of life but his mum decided against the doctors' advice. And he is very grateful for that. In the other guy's case, he went through it with his wife. She could have died, if she had given birth. So they decided to abort the baby.'

'Wow, that's a horrifying experience,' said Helen, looking at her sister's eyes and listening carefully to every word she said.

'Yes, I know. They are suffering. Both of them. It is so hard to find a starting point for this kind of discussion if your experiences are so dramatically different from each other.'

'Yeah, it is not easy. So what is your plan now?' Helen asked.

'Both of them will be coming to New York shortly for some UN session or other. I will chat with them again. Just need some time to prepare,' Conny responded.

'With milk and sugar?' Mary interrupted suddenly.

'Yes, please.' Conny responded.

'No sugar, only milk,' Helen added.

Given where Mary was working and what she was involved in, she was a very old-school type of person. No self-driving car and no automated coffee machine. Making coffee like a professional barista was much more fun, and she had never wanted this experience to be taken from her. Because you cannot take everything from your life that is not efficient or productive enough in the eyes of today's life coaches. Some things are done just for fun and entertainment.

'What about your first week of school?' Mary asked Helen while bringing coffee to the table.

'Good so far.' Helen didn't really want to go into too many details. 'Spoiled kids with teenager problems. I can see some suffering there as well. What about your trip, Mary? I guess it went well, if you had to stay longer,' Helen asked and changed the focus from herself to Mary.

'It went ok, I guess. I don't think that there is a standard for how this should look. It was very difficult to get into the UN HQ and meet with that person. She is pretty high up there. Some kind of commissioner. She was trying to be very politically correct when we talked together.'

'Ok. So not much luck with her?' Helen followed up.

'Actually, not really. I think I got somewhere with her. She has a family, but also a lover.'

'Wow, this is getting spicy now,' Helen commented with a smile.

'I know, right?' Mary smiled as well. 'Life is never boring. Everyone has those secrets that can ruin your life when revealed. At the same time these motivate you to wake up when ordinary everyday duties seem to have buried all the fun.'

'Did she tell you that she has a lover?' Helen asked.

'Of course not … I followed her. And this man is in the hospital, on his deathbed. Suffering a lot. He has some kind of disease I can't even pronounce.'

'Did you talk to her about that?' Helen asked.

'Yes, this is why I stayed longer. I feel bad for her. She is thinking about euthanasia, but she also loves him so much that she doesn't want to let him go. She might be coming to the same conference as Conny's buddies. We'll see.'

'That's good, I guess. You might be able to complete your mission quickly.' Helen said, thinking that her mission might be a bit more complex after all.

5

Helen felt a bit anxious while walking to work on Monday morning. Luckily enough she didn't have to meet the 'curious' class until lunchtime, so she could at least enjoy a quiet morning. But then she ran into Jane.

'Hi Jane, how are you?'

'Hello Ms Murphy. I'm good.' Jane's voice wasn't too convincing.

'Is everything alright?' Helen asked. There was this thought that had come into Helen's mind again over the weekend that all this might relate to Jane's own problem and that she just wanted to get some answers to her own issues.

'Yeah, I guess so,' Jane answered quickly. 'Do you have a sec?'

'Sure, let's go to a classroom.' Helen pointed out the nearest one and they went in.

'We did it. He asked me to have sex with him. Threatened that he would leave me if we didn't do it. And left me at the end, because he said I was terrible at sex,' said Jane as soon as the door shut. She started crying.

'Oh dear.' Helen hugged her. 'You are just 17,' Helen whispered.

'Have you told your parents?' Helen asked, not knowing why.

'God, no. My dad would kill me, and my mum would not stop crying,' Jane mumbled through her tears.

'By any chance, do you have a break at 12?' Helen asked politely.

'Yes, until 1 p.m. We have a history class with you then, Ms Murphy,' Jane responded.

'Great, so you want to grab lunch somewhere outside?' Helen asked again and put a hand on her shoulder.

'Okay. I'm sorry Ms Murphy. I have no one else I can tell this to,' Jane was still crying.

'No reason to apologise. This is just life stuff.' Helen had already started to think about what she could say to her. It was not a topic she felt very confident speaking about. For the next few hours Helen could not stop thinking about it. 'Maybe this is why I got this particular mission. Very strange,' she thought. This was definitely not something Helen had expected. She had expected more questions related to history, but not those difficult life questions, which she was having a hard time answering herself, never mind being a guide for a little woman.

'Dad, if you can hear me now, help me, please. I really don't know what I should say,' she thought. She was very nervous when she left the school with Jane. She calmed down with the first bite she took of a chicken sandwich.

'Chicken doesn't taste like it used to, years ago.' Helen started to cut the tension related to this uncomfortable situation.

'Tastes the same as usual to me,' Jane responded.

Yeah, you have probably never tasted a real chicken that walked freely on earth.' Helen smiled, hoping that would cheer Jane up a bit. But Jane was quiet.

'So what really happened last night?' Helen started the proper conversation.

'Brian came back from college, and we had a bite to eat. Then my parents left for the evening to have their anniversary dinner and we were left alone. And Brian said to me that he thinks that I don't love him and this is why I don't want to have sex with him. He added that he has his needs, which he cannot control, and needs to do something about because otherwise he will explode. He finished by saying that he didn't want to leave me but had no choice because I was thinking only about myself.' Jane started weeping a bit.

'Wow, where did you find him? He sounds like a douchebag … I don't want to use a worse word here.' Helen winked. Helen herself didn't have much experience with men, but still she hoped that one day she would find 'the one'.

'You mean … 'asshole'? Yes, he is a total asshole.'

'And you agreed?' Helen asked

'Unfortunately, yes. I didn't see any other choice. I loved him … but he treated me like a sex toy, and I think I'm pregnant. I can't have a baby now.' Jane started crying again,

'And then he left?' Helen asked.

'Yes, he said that it was the worst experience he had ever had, and it seems that we are not a good match for sex either, so he doesn't see any future in this relationship.'

'Wow, that's a very dumb and rude statement. What an asshole!' Helen couldn't believe what Jane was saying. She was eight years older than Jane, so she couldn't behave like a mother in this situation, more like a friend.

'I know, right? What should I do now?' Jane asked, hoping for some life-saving advice from Helen. But sometimes things are so complicated that it is not easy to give advice.

'Hmm … Well, what about talking to the school counsellor?'

'Is this really all you've got for me?' Jane got a bit angry. 'The school counsellor is well paid by my family. She would run directly to my father and I would be screwed forever! I thought you were different!' she shouted and stood up.

'I am,' said Helen quietly. 'Sit down, I will tell you my story.' Helen smiled shyly. She didn't really see any other option than to open herself to this vulnerable girl in front of her. She thought that maybe explaining to Jane what her own experiences had been would help Jane to understand the dynamics of building relationships and the risks related to it.

'Where to start?' she paused for a moment. 'I had a difficult time in my life. My parents were killed in 2030, and to be frank, we didn't get good publicity as a family at the time. My sisters and I were split between different foster families, and we didn't have much hope for ourselves. I met this boy at a party, when I was in college. At that time, I was really involved in cheerleading, parties, and so on. Then we started dating and it was great. Until at one party-' Helen paused again, like all the memories were coming back to her. 'Nothing crazy. Just close friends. Me, my boyfriend, his mate and my best friend. Long story short. His friend raped me in front of him.' She paused one more time and put her head down. She didn't want to go into details. This was not the point of this story. 'No one stopped him. My best friend, Courtney, was afraid to say anything, at least that's what I hope,' she put her head down again, looking at the floor. 'My boyfriend was happy to share me with his mate, like I was a toy. He was having a great time. Enjoying just watching,' she closed her eyes. It was so difficult to look into Jane's face. 'I felt so humiliated.'

'Wow, this story is even more messed up than mine,' Jane quickly commented.

'Hmm … thank you?!' Helen tried to smile. 'We should go back to school.'

'Yeah, let's go.' Jane felt a bit better knowing that her story wasn't the worst possible scenario. Helen, on the other hand, felt a bit weird knowing that she had told her biggest secret to a 17-year-old girl she didn't even know. But it was done now. No turning back. Strangely enough she also felt relief. She had been holding this secret in for so long that it had become very heavy in her heart, and telling someone removed it from her chest.

'Last class today, let's finish this Monday, finally.' Helen tried to encourage herself while she was walking to the classroom, where the 'curious' class was already waiting. Unfortunately, the class didn't let her off the hook too easily. This was definitely not something Helen had been expecting. The question from Friday came back. And while Helen was trying to get around answering the question, Jane came out and shared some of the most shocking details from the story Helen had just told her. Helen couldn't really say anything. She just stood and stared into space. Some girls in the class smiled at her with pity while some laughed, thinking about what a loser they had for a teacher. Helen wasn't sure if a moment of kindness would have made her feel better. Class was over. The day was over. All of the kids left the classroom.

Jane didn't seem to actually understand what she had done in that moment. And that was very common for this generation. They couldn't understand. They were incapable of getting it, because they didn't really know what it meant to have a relationship with another person and how to care for it. They looked at their social life from another perspective, that of online presence. Helen's life didn't matter because she was not very vocal online, she was not there, where everyone else was. For this generation, there was no 'be', just 'have'. People have a life, relationships and social profiles. They had raised a generation that was incapable of building a friendship with any other human being. They looked only for the highlights in life, rather than the whole story. They were a generation whose understanding of human relationships was based on pop culture values. The Third World has not killed everyone and everything, but you cannot kill something that is already dead. And humankind had been killed at the root of its nature – in people's ability to form relationships.

Helen went back home. Anyone who met her on the street, on her way back, might have thought that she was in another world. She was quiet, her eyes were still staring at something invisible. She barely moved her head. The weather in New York that day was great but you couldn't actually see if she was enjoying it or not. She wasn't present. She was somewhere back there, in her painful memories, in the events that had happened six years ago.

She felt like she had jumped back into the depressed state she had been trying to get off for years, and finally started managing it a few months ago. She was now right back in that state. The state when you feel unworthy of living in this world. The state when every brief look from another person humiliates you. The state when you can't cry anymore, because you feel that the tears you have already cried would make a decent-sized lake overflow, there had been so many of them. But this time it was a bit different. She wasn't alone in this world, she had her sisters.

She got back to the apartment and opened the door. Conny was sitting on the couch. She didn't look at her at first.

'Hey Sis, you're back early?!' Conny said. There was no response. Conny lifted her eyes to look at Helen.

'Rough day, hey?' she asked. And then suddenly Helen burst in tears.

'Oh dear,' said Conny. She hadn't been in this situation before. She got her cell phone, and called Mary. 'Hey Mary, we have a situation and I think I need you here,' she said quickly over the phone. She hung up after Mary confirmed that she would come over as soon as she could. Then she walked over to Helen and hugged her. She didn't really know what to do. She knew though that this cry wasn't an easy, quick problem to be solved, so she just said: 'You will be alright, Sis. You are not alone.'

Mary got to Helen's pretty quickly. She avoided rush hour because she left the office early. And then they were all there. All three, sitting on the couch. Helen was in the middle, and Mary and Conny on each side of her.

'Thank you,' said Helen with her sad voice. No worries, Sis! said Conny in response. Conny and Mary patiently waited until Helen was able to speak.

'I haven't seen her in that state before,' said Mary to Conny while they were making tea in the kitchen. It sounded a bit weird, considering that she hadn't been in touch with any of her sisters for years, but at the same time she was right in this case. This was a very unusual situation for Helen. Most days Helen was very cheerful, maybe hiding pain and sadness, because we know that everyone has those days. But she was really good at pretending. But now, all these defences had come down and she was truly herself.

After ninety minutes of silence, weeping and crying, Helen finally started talking. She told them her story, which no one really knew about. She spoke slowly, weighing every word and feeling again the pain she had felt in her chest that day. She also explained in detail what had happened at school that day and why she had come home from work earlier. After listening to her full story, Mary called Simone. They wanted to keep her in the loop. They were back together, more secrets could damage what they were trying to rebuild.

Simone made a very important decision that evening. She went to Logan airport and caught a flight to New York. Simone herself was probably surprised by her reaction. Something was changing in her. She missed her sisters, she needed friends and naturally Mary, Helen and Conny seemed to be the best candidates for that role.

When Helen finished her speech, there was silence. Neither Mary nor Conny saw a reason to speak up. It wasn't a good moment to play the smartass, and they were also empathetic. They knew that this had really hurt their sister's heart.

'She is such an innocent girl,' said Conny to Mary quietly. Just around 9 p.m., Mary stood up in front of Helen. She raised her chin so she could look directly into her eyes.

'Helen, you are the strongest person I know. You can get over it. And we are here to help you. We will carry that cross with you!' Mary hugged her. Conny joined them.

Helen started crying even more when she heard Mary's speech. It is like you think it cannot get worse than this drama, and then seconds later it gets worse.

'I got pregnant, too,' Helen said out of the blue. 'And I aborted my child because my boyfriend wanted me to.' She started crying even more. 'I can't forget about this child. I think about him every day.' Conny and Mary were barely able to understand what she was saying with her sad and sobbing voice.

This was like a new layer of problems. Mary decided to stay overnight. There was not much to talk about. These topics were too difficult to digest for even the most intelligent and strong people.

Around 1 a.m. Simone arrived. When Helen saw her, she burst into tears again. 'You didn't have to come,' said Helen, in her tearful voice.

'Of course, I had to. You are my sister. You are not alone. You would do the same for me.' And she hugged her. In all of that sadness, during this difficult time, Helen was not alone. And as much as she would have liked to be in a better place, she was glad that at least this had brought them all together again.

Helen was not able to go to school that week. She needed time off. Simone stayed for a few days with her and Conny. It was good for all of them. To learn something about each other. They had missed out on a few years of each other's lives. They were now starting to rebuild this bond that had been between them before. Even Mary took some time off and joined them. They were happy times, encouraging for everyone, especially for Helen. It was nice to not think about her difficult life story or what had happened at school. They spent their time baking, telling old stories from their childhood or just talking about each other's lives and it was relaxing for Helen.

Eventually though, they had to touch on the topic again. Helen had to go back to school the following week and her sisters needed to go back to their own jobs.

'How are you feeling, Helen? asked Mary, out of the blue while they were watching a funny movie from their childhood.

'It is so good to have you all here. You really made things easier for me. For so long I was alone with this,' Helen paused for a moment. 'And you can't solve this problem for me. No, that's my cross, and I will be carrying it for the rest of my life. But you are helping me to carry it.' Helen smiled and tears ran down her cheeks.

'We didn't do a thing, Helen! We probably don't even know how to fix your problems. We all have some issues, which we can't really sort out,' Conny admitted.

'You are here for me. That's enough. There is no easy fix for this. I need to work through this. Inside me,' Helen said.

'What about school? Are you going back?' Simone asked.

'I can't run away from those questions. There is a reason why Dad put me in this place. I cannot forget that I have a mission to complete. It won't be easy, but I need to pull myself together and go back on Monday.'

'Brave girl!' Mary shouted.

'Listen, Helen, I will have to leave for the airport now … I don't want to miss my flight. I hope Marcus fed Francis sometimes,' Simone laughed.

'Thank you so much Simone for coming. It was so kind. I promise that I will visit you soon.' Helen kissed and hugged Simone.

'Would be great if you could meet my family. I told Francis about all of you, he can't wait to meet his aunties. Okay. It is time to leave. Bye girls.' Simone kissed her sisters, took her luggage and left the apartment.

'Safe journey!' shouted Mary. 'Listen Helen, I have to go shortly as well. On Saturday we usually have a movie night and I already missed last week's '

'Of course Mary. Thank you once again for your time. Say hello to John and Eugene.' Helen kissed Mary.

'Bye Conny, I will chat with you on Monday. We need to sort out this thing with the UN conference.' Mary winked at Conny.

'Sure thing, Sis, talk to you soon,' responded Conny. Mary left. Conny and Helen were left alone again.

'Are you really ok?' Conny asked Helen.

'Yes, I think so. I will probably never be ok with what I have done with my child … but, well … I can't really turn back time,' Helen responded.

'And on top of all that, my mission is about abortion … sorry, Sis, I will try not to mention it,' Conny said.

'No. Talk about it. I want to share this with you. I want to help you to understand what was happening in me before and after that happened.' Helen looked into Conny's eyes seriously.

'You sure? I don't want to hurt you more,' Conny was not convinced.

'You can't hurt me more. But we can learn something from it together and try to save some lives in the future.' Helen smiled.

'Ok. Let's get something to eat first. I'm starving!' Conny concluded.

***

Simone got home just after 10 p.m. Marcus was not asleep yet. He was waiting for her. Sitting in his favourite chair.

'You are finally home!' he shouted. He seemed to be very angry.

'Sorry honey, it took longer than I thought. Helen was not feeling well at all.' Simone tried to calm down the situation.

'So, your sisters show up, out of the blue, and you are leaving your family, and don't care about your motherly duties anymore?' he asked.

'I don't think that is a fair statement, Marcus. I tried to be the best mother I could be for Francis, for so many years. I was away for a few days.' Simone was still calm.

'What about me? You know that it is not my job to take care of our son. You are a stay-at-home mother. It is your responsibility. I'm doing a real job and earning money so you can spend it on your needs.' Marcus was clearly attacking Simone.

'Listen to yourself … I'm not sure what you want me to say here,' Simone replied while she busied herself with unpacking.

'You should apologise and make up for this. And I don't want to hear about your sisters anymore.' Marcus sounded serious.

'Are you serious?' Simone started laughing.

'Yes, I am. I won't tolerate this kind of behaviour.' Marcus left the room. Simone was shocked by Marcus' allegations and threats. She thought maybe he had had a rough time with Francis and was just tired. She was going to check up on Francis when she suddenly got a text.

'Who could that be?' she thought. The message was from Claire: 'Can we meet now? The same place as before.'

'Ok,' she responded quickly. 'Greg's wife? I wonder what she might be looking for,' she whispered to herself. Simone didn't think about it for too long. 'I guess Marcus reacted this way, because some things never change in people,' she thought to herself. She just ignored him. Marcus probably thought the same thing. He had told her where her place was, and he was now expecting her behaviour to improve. But this time was different. Simone's world had started to expand. Marcus and Francis were not the only people in her life anymore. Simone quickly put her shoes back on, checked on Franky and left the apartment. She didn't really know what to expect from Claire, but it was still better than sitting in the bed with grumpy Marcus.

She met Claire in a bar, ten minutes from her apartment block. She didn't look well. She was wearing sunglasses and was very nervous.

'Hey Claire, how are you? Is everything ok?' Simone asked politely.

'Not really, look at this!' Claire took off her glasses and Simone could see her swollen right eye.

'What happened?' Simone asked, worried about her.

'What do you think?' Claire responded.

'Did Greg hit you?' Simone asked.

'Yes, he did, yesterday. We had an argument about some stupid thing, I don't even remember what it was and then he hit me. He lost his temper, big time.' Claire was angry and scared at the same time.

'Have you gone to the police? Or at least the hospital? It might be serious.' Simone was worried about her.

'I will be fine. Don't worry. The police would not help me. He is well known in Boston. They can't touch him. But you are a freelance journalist, you can tell the story about the real Greg O'Donnell. That would hurt him.' Claire was thinking about some evil revenge plan.

'With all due respect, you might not have a winning case here. Your word against his.' Simone, knowing that she was not a real journalist, was trying to get out of this situation.

'I get it. Sure. But what if I can get some documents about this project, GD1, that I was telling you about?' Claire asked.

'Oh yeah. I remember. I checked online, there was nothing controversial about it,' Simone stated.

'Yeah, not everything is available to public eyes.' Claire smiled evilly. 'Usually some of those documents have side notes that specifically describe people's real intentions,' she added.

'Ok. We can have a look. Are you really ok?' Simone asked again.

'I'm not ok because this asshole really pissed me off this time. We had argued before. And I know that we were not the perfect couple. But he raised his hand to me, he hit me. I will chop that hand off the next time he raises it! I have to go now. I will get you those docs. Bye!' Claire put her sunglasses back on and left the bar.

'Do you want to order something?' the bartender asked suddenly.

'No, I'm good. I don't think you have anything strong enough for this.' Simone laughed and left the bar as well. She thought about this conversation with Claire on the way back home. 'And yeah, about this Marcus thing,' she thought to herself. 'He would never raise a hand on me,' she tried to convince herself. She decided to give him a bit more time to get over this whole thing. 'We are only humans,' she defended him to herself.

The next day it seemed like everything had gone back to how it had been before. Marcus wasn't so cranky anymore and he even smiled a bit. He wasn't too cheerful, but she guessed that was just not his thing. The day was passing peacefully when Simone received some documents in an email from Claire. Marcus took Francis to watch the Red Sox play the Giants, so Simone had time to have a quick look. These seemed to be some of the internal notes that had been created during team meetings. It looked like the team was working on the GD1 project and the motivations of the team members were pretty clear. Funnily enough, considering that this was related to gender inequality, those meetings had involved only male project team members. In the email, Claire explained that women were only added later so they could provide feedback and execute the whole thing.

'This is not what Greg was talking about,' Simone said quietly. While she was still going through the documents, Claire sent her another email, just an hour after the first one. It simply said: 'I think Greg figured out that I have stolen these documents. Print them out before the online copies disappear.'

Simone had to think for a second about how to print them out. She hadn't used the printer for years, but she knew that Marcus had a printer, as he had occasionally had to print out some legal documents. She found the printer in his office and printed off eighty pages and brought them to her bedroom. 'Looks like I will have a nice bedtime story to read,' she thought. In the meantime she had received another text from Claire. 'Hide those docs well. I think Greg wants to attack me first so this will not get released'

That got Simone thinking. 'Why did I even get into this? It seems like Claire is in so much shit, and I'm not even the person she thinks I am. I don't even know how to fix this.' Exhausted from all of that stress, Simone fell asleep. She didn't even hear when Marcus and Francis came back. She woke up when Marcus stormed into the bedroom shouting: 'What the fuck is this shit?!' He was holding a piece of paper in his hand.

'What?' Simone was confused and sleepy, she couldn't open her eyes.

'I tried to print something and there was no paper. I was surprised. I added more paper to the printer and this printed. Some confidential documents from the company I'm representing!' He couldn't calm down.

'I don't know what you are talking about.' Simone was only slowly coming back to reality after having been asleep.

'Oh … don't lie to me again. I know you, you lazy bitch! At the same time that Greg from this firm is emailing me to say that he wants to sue his wife and get divorced from her! What the fuck is going on? What the heck were you doing?' He had really lost his temper.

'Greg Donnelly?' she asked

'How do you know him?! How did you get those confidential docs?' Marcus was still shouting. Simone stood up.

'Why are you shouting? You will scare Francis.' She said it very calmly.

'I don't give a shit. This is not about our son, it is about you doing something to break up this family and ruin my life!' He sounded very frustrated.

'Your life? What about my life?' Simone was beginning to lose her temper too.

'You are my wife, and you should be doing what I tell you to do! I work hard to take care of this family and you. You should thank me for that, not destroy my career!'

'Just listen to yourself!' This was probably the first time Simone had started to lose patience with him since she'd started dating him.

'Shut up. Stop doing whatever you are doing that is related to Greg or his company … if you don't,' he paused for a moment.

'If I don't, what? Are you threatening me?' she asked

'You will regret it … I will leave and I will leave all this shit behind and you will have to take care of yourself and Francis … we will see if you feel so smart then.' Marcus left the room and shut the door.

Simone started crying. 'What have I done?' she asked herself. 'What should I do now? What about Francis?' All these thoughts were going around her head. This was one of those moments when you tried to do something different, outside of your daily routine, and you felt how painful it was. People don't accept you changing or being different from what you usually are. On the one hand that discourages you, massively, but on the other hand you know that taking that step was a huge decision for you and you don't want to turn back. She went to the living room, where Marcus was sitting on the couch.

'You can't talk to me that way!' she shouted at him.

'What? You owe me.' He stood up.

'I do not owe you shit!' She tried to stand up for herself. Marcus slapped her right cheek.

'I won't be repeating myself,' he said with a calm and strong voice. 'Listen to me, and stop playing dumb. I told you what you will do. You will drop this case, keep away from this case. It is not your business!' Marcus left the room again. He left the apartment. Simone was standing there, shocked. He hit her. Her husband hit her. The one who loved her so much. It was like a wake-up call. It was a new reality.

'I've been treated like an object, with no feelings, no rights, no opinions.' She was mad, scared and annoyed at the same time. 'What should I do now?' she asked herself.

'Why are you crying, Mum?' A little boy's voice sounded in the empty room.

'Because I'm sad,' she responded, weeping quietly

'Don't cry, Mum. You are a good person. Good people don't have reasons to cry.' The boy smiled and hugged her. She started crying even more. 'I have to do something,' she thought. I cannot leave this situation like this. She called Helen and decided to move in with her with Francis for the time being. She packed up, closed the door, and left for the airport with Francis.

***

In the meantime, Conny and Mary met up to discuss the next steps to take with the people from Zurich.

'I have actually already scheduled a meeting with Karl for tomorrow, he got here earlier to meet up with his teenage daughter who lives with her mother here,' said Conny, sipping a coffee.

'Oh, that's great. I don't think my lady will be here so soon. I remember that she told me that she is not very keen on travelling. She has to do it sometimes, but it is not something she enjoys very much. Also, her mind is probably on other things.' Mary was finishing her coffee.

'Do you want to go for a walk or something? It is nice outside and we can take Eugene and John …'

Conny paused for a moment. 'I can't get used to sitting at home all the time. I was homeless for years, remember?' she smiled.

'Yeah, sure. Let's go.' Mary stood up. As they were going down the stairs, a door on the first floor suddenly opened.

'Hi!' said a young male voice.

'Hi!' responded Mary. 'You are new here, right? Welcome!' she added.

'Yes, I have just moved in,' he responded. 'Your voice sounds familiar, do I know you?'

'My name is Mary, and this is Conny, my husband Eugene, and my son, John.' Mary pointed out all the people she was with.

'Oh … Mary, Conny – sounds familiar. There were more of you, right? Helen? Susan?' He tried to remember.

'Yeah, Helen and Simone,'. Mary corrected him.

'Yes, Simone. Sorry,' he responded.

'How do you know us?' Conny asked. She wasn't able to figure out who this guy was.

'Oh sorry, I'm Kevin Stinson,' he responded quickly.

'Stinson? That rings a bell. I had a friend at my school, Margaret Stinson,' Mary responded.

'Yep, that's my sister.' Kevin smiled.

'Oh, wow. Small world. I didn't know that she had a brother.' Mary was curious.

'She is twelve years older than me. And I was sick when I was a baby so I didn't go out much.'

'Wow, ok. What are you doing here?' Conny asked.

'Just started my studies. Where are you going? Don't want to hold you up for too long.' He smiled.

'Just going to the park,' Mary responded.

'Ok. Cool. Let me grab a jumper and I will get some coffee with you.' He turned around and quickly picked up his jumper. He walked with them for a good twenty minutes. He was a very interesting boy. He didn't know the sisters personally, from what he was saying, but from the stories he had heard about this mysterious family of criminals, as he called them. He wanted to understand more about what had happened to their parents and what they believed in and he also told them what he thought about today's world. He was impressed how easy the world had become for humans. Technology, AI, medicine, robots. Life was easy. Great companies were trying to bring humankind to the next level and help people to develop and give them better opportunities. He felt that finally it was all about him, about human beings. Everything was focused on his needs, and he felt satisfied with this. Equality between people. Gender equality. He could choose for himself if he wanted to be heterosexual or homosexual. He could fully decide for himself and be happy. Unhappiness had been removed from this world, at least for many people.

Mary and Conny listened to him carefully, and he made a lot of sense. But at the same time there was something scary in what he was saying. When he left, they chatted about how they could solve the problems of those people their missions were related to. And they promised themselves that they would do everything to help each other, because this is what sisters should do.

In the evening, Mary started reflecting on her own life and situation. In some ways, her situation was pretty similar to that of the woman from the UN. Not exactly, obviously, but in some ways: the person who she loved the most was sick. She started understanding why Dad had given her that mission. It was not the only mission to be completed. Her life needed to be fixed as well. And that mission was even more important.

6

Helen woke up with a headache and thought to herself that the weather was probably about to change. She got some painkillers and grabbed some coffee. Yep. It was 2037 but painkillers and coffee remained the best solution for a blurry morning. Constance wasn't home, she had meant to go for a jog and then meet with Mary again.

'I know what might cheer me up,' Helen said to herself. 'Our old family house … that's what I need.' She smiled to herself. She put on some comfortable clothes, grabbed a quick bite to eat and left the apartment. The car was already waiting for her outside. The journey didn't take long. She smiled brightly when she saw the house again. So many good memories. She regretted that she hadn't done this more often.

She entered quickly and walked around. She touched things, looked at the pictures and photographs on the walls and tried to remember stories about them. So many things had happened here. She went to her room and lay down on the dusty bed. The dust made her start coughing. 'I guess this was not the best idea.' She got up very quickly. She sat down on a chair and just looked around. 'I really loved that room,' she said quietly.

'My own room, where I could do what I wanted to do. I could just close the door, and I could get away from the whole world. Great times. I have no place to hide like that anymore.' She stood up, and decided to go back to the attic. She left the room, closed the door, and climbed the wooden stairs to the attic. It looked the same as when they had left it 'Weird, it is not as dusty as my room. I don't remember cleaning this place up when we were here last time,' she said to herself.

She sat down on the couch to see if the mysterious voice from the last visit would start talking again. No, it was quiet. She spent a few minutes on the couch, and then got up and walked around the attic. As kids they had never really spent time there. It was Dad's workplace. He was always doing something here. Helen wasn't even sure what exactly. Reading? Writing? Praying? On the old brown wooden desk there was a picture. She took it. 'Wow,' she thought. 'We are all in this. Even Mary. Probably Dad's birthday, just before Mary left home. One big happy family.' She smiled. She opened the window and sat down in her dad's favourite rocking chair. She looked at the picture again, trying to remember how she had felt at the time. 'I miss you all so much. Mum, Dad … I'm such a mess. It would be great to hear your advice now,' she said directly to the picture, hoping that they could somehow hear her. She started weeping and tears started to fall on the picture. She hugged it. 'I really need your help. I don't know what to do. I have no clue how I can talk to those kids tomorrow.'

She closed her eyes. At this point she was even tired thinking about scenarios of what might happen tomorrow. How could she handle it, how could she handle herself? She knew that those girls were not the problem. They were just curious. She knew that she could help them. But at the same time this was something she didn't know how to even approach. Because she felt she was not the right person to do this kind of thing. She was weak. This whole situation was overwhelming for her. For years she had been trying to escape from it, and now she had to stand up and confront the problem that was really inside her. She felt ugly, she felt disgusting when she thought about sex, about being a woman. Someone who can be used like an object, looked at as someone who only satisfies men's sexual needs. It was so dehumanising to her. She needed someone to tell her that she was beautiful again, that her existence was about more than being a woman. She needed someone she trusted and respected, like her father, who used to tell her that she was a lovely, beautiful woman. She fell asleep in the chair eventually and spent at least two hours on it.

'You are the most beautiful creature I created!' she heard in her heart suddenly.

'Dad, are you here?' She immediately opened her eyes. She felt this warm feeling in her heart. Like someone was hugging her. Like Mum, or Dad. She heard those words in her heart over and over again. Maybe it was just her unconscious that was trying to convince her of that truth about herself. But she had experienced this before; many times after that hurtful episode she had tried to convince herself that everything was going to be alright. She wanted to think positively about herself and this world. This time it was different, it was coming from inside her. She did not say anything. The thought came to her heart and spread across her body, warming it up. She felt indescribable courage. It was like a gust of wind that blew away everything that was hurtful and damaging and brought peace to her heart, and courage. She smiled. 'Let's do something about it,' she shouted to herself and stood up. She picked up her phone and called Conny.

'Hey Constance! How are you doing? I will need your help. Are you going to be home later?' she asked quickly

'Yeah, will be back at 8 p.m. Let's chat then.' Conny didn't know what to expect but was happy to hear the excitement and happiness in Helen's voice over the phone.

'Sounds good. Talk to you later.' Helen had a plan in her head, and she needed her sister to help out with it.

***

In the meantime, Conny and Mary had agreed on the tactics for their missions. Conny was planning to confront both sides and discuss with them the options for common ground. Mary was planning to meet the woman and be very frank about her life, and what she was trying to achieve here. And she did meet her hours later. UN Commissioner, Lisa, was not a bad person, just confused, like many people those days were. It was difficult to choose goodness when the definition of good is relative. And all of the options look good from the outside. After the second coffee, Mary opened up a bit. This was her strategy to get this woman to open up as well. 'My husband is paralysed. And it's totally my fault,' she said unexpectedly to the older lady.

'How come?' she responded, surprised.

'I thought he was cheating on me.' She felt ashamed saying it. 'That evening I thought he was going to her, so I left John with our nanny and followed him. It was dark. He hadn't seen me, but he got nervous, and lost control of the car. He hit a tree just outside of town.' Mary had tears in her eyes.

'Was he cheating on you?' the woman asked, trying to help Mary justify what had happened.

'No. He was actually preparing something for our wedding anniversary …' Mary cried.

'Oh, that's sad.' The woman didn't know how to respond to that.

'I was obsessed. It was my fault. But I still love him so much. And it is not a guilty love. We adopted a child together. He is a father, I'm a mother. We are a family.' Mary was saying all of this from the depths of her heart.

'Why are you telling me all of that? Because of the UN resolution? The lady was getting a bit curious.

'Yes and no,' she responded.

'What do you mean? We already talked about the resolution. People should have a choice about their lives – if they don't see the point in staying alive and are simply suffering, they should have the freedom to end it, or someone close to their family should have this choice.'

'Let me take you somewhere not far from here,' Mary said.

'I don't have time. Sorry, but we should be wrapping up this conversation here.' The commissioner stood up. 'I have to be going now, you can't just waste more of my time.'

'Wait. I didn't want to play this game but you are giving me no choice. I know about your lover, I know where you sneak out to in the evenings,' Mary said with a poker face.

'Well ok, where did you want to bring me?' the woman asked, not continuing the conversation about her secret. 'Just remember, I won't be threatened by anyone.'

'That is not my plan. Let's go to my apartment.' Mary stood up and went out through the door. The woman followed her.

Eugene was sitting in his wheelchair as usual and looking out the window. His gaze seemed vacant. Sometimes Mary thought that his soul was not there. The accident had paralysed him, but even more, it had killed something inside him. Killed life in him. Mary didn't know if he knew that it was her fault. Eugene had been a very talented doctor, with a great career ahead of him. Mary knew that, and she was someone who really understood the importance of having a career. What if he could have been incredible in his role, and had been able to save thousands of lives? She wondered about it sometimes. And then she was always upset, because she had killed that dream of his, and almost killed him. That she was so suspicious and emotional and had somehow led to this tragedy. She felt responsible for him. She was not free from guilt, and she felt pity for him. She wanted to compensate for what she had done. At the same time, she was always moved when John went to Eugene. Eugene obviously couldn't play with his son, but you could see that he moved his eyes. He was happy when he saw him, and in some mystical way John understood and felt that his daddy was present and was playing with him, in this awkward way.

The woman was looking at him, and thinking about her lover who could not move at all. 'But don't you think that he is suffering? That he would prefer to not be alive?' she asked Mary.

'Is quality of life more important than life itself? I love both of them. I understand how much pain he went through and probably he suffers mentally every day knowing that his life will not change. At the same time, I know how big a gift his life is to me and John. And I truly believe that he thinks about my life and his son's life as gifts to him, which helps him to live.' Mary was moved because that was also an answer to her own questions.

'So what do you want me to do?' The commissioner asked.

'I want you to look at the person you love, and truly, from the depths of your heart, answer this question. Is it really going to be easier for you and for him, if he ends his life? This is not just an escape from suffering. That's an easy answer to a complex question. But an answer that is not love, because love is more than suffering, problems, quality of life. Love is life, love is an existence with eternal purpose.' The woman checked her watch. She was not moved as much as Mary, or at least she didn't show it too much.

'I have to go now. I have some evening meetings. Goodbye.' She turned around, went out through the hall and left the apartment.

'Bye,' Mary cried out at the end. 'I hope she is just playing this though woman with no feelings,' Mary thought as she sat on the couch.

***

'I can't just leave it that way,' thought Simone on her way to the airport. 'Francis, let me drop you at Aunt Elaine's for a few hours, I need to sort out some things.'

'Ok Mum. Is Jack going to be there as well?' Francis asked about his little cousin.

'Don't know, Frank. We'll see,' Simone responded to her son. The car changed direction and went to Aunt Elaine's house in Cambridge. Simone didn't know what to do exactly, but she had the feeling that she couldn't leave this whole situation like this. Once she had left Frank with her aunt, she decided to go to Greg. She texted Claire and got their home address. Claire responded that she was not home, but Simone didn't want to talk to her. She wanted to meet Greg, face to face.

They had a beautiful house in Cambridge. It was a two-storey building, with plenty of room. They didn't have kids, so Simone was surprised by the size of it.

It was getting a bit dark outside, and she put her hoodie on. 'He'll definitely have some cameras up in front of his house, he will never let me in if he sees me,' she thought. Simone rang the doorbell. No one answered via camera, but she heard someone walking to the door. The door opened.

'Hi, how can I help you?' Greg said to Simone, but did not recognise her.

'Hi Greg, I need to talk to you,' Simone answered straight away, and started walking in.

'Please come in,' Greg was surprised by her behaviour. 'Who are you and how can I help you?' The door had been shut after her.

'I wanted to talk with you about your wife,' Simone said.

'What? My wife? I remember you now. You are that freelance journalist. I will have to ask you to leave my house,' Greg demanded.

'No. You must listen to me. I know that you hit your wife. I also know what kind of work on gender equality you are doing in your company,' Simone started saying. She had this idea that if she told him everything she knew, he would be scared and would change his life, apologise to his wife, leave the job and be a good man. Utopian. But it was nice to have some hope for a few minutes at least.

'What? That is not true. My wife lied to you,' Greg tried to defend himself.

'No. I saw her eye …'

'She fell on the stairs,' Greg was quick to come up with an excuse.

'Bullshit. I have seen your internal documents.' Simone wanted to hurt him more.

'What? That's confidential. You stole them, I'm going to call the police,' Greg started threatening her.

'Don't be so quick with that, you little shit.' Simone started losing her cool.

'Why are you calling me names?' Greg was surprised by her reaction.

'Everyone who beats women is a little, cowardly shit to me,' Simone was fuming with anger.

'Ok … could you leave this house, now.' Greg was getting annoyed.

'Listen to me, you'd better fix your issues with Claire or the documents are going to be released on the internet and your career will be finished.' Simone didn't want to waste more time with him.

'Are you threatening me with stolen documents? Seriously? No one will believe you. And you will go to jail.' Greg was very confident.

'Bring it on mate, we will see what will hurt whom first. You know that if something is posted on the internet it never disappears,' said Simone, playing her game. She felt very confident, like she held all the aces. Greg turned around and started walking towards the window. 'I hope he doesn't grab a knife and kill me here,' Simone thought. He stopped at the window and looked out at his garden for a moment. Then he turned around and said: 'All right. So be it. I will sort it out with Claire, but in return I will ask you to return all the copies of the documents you have.' Greg was thinking of a strategy.

'Sure. Claire will give them to you when she feels satisfied with how you have fixed your issues. And by the way … I'm not a freelance journalist …' Simone turned around and went to the door.

'What the heck, so who are you?' Greg shouted. But the answer never came. Simone left the house and went to Elaine to pick up Francis.

'We might even be able to catch the last flight to JFK,' she said to herself. She felt relieved. She had finally been able to help someone. She had stood up for this woman. It felt great and she smiled the whole way back to New York. 'Was that meant to be my mission?' she wondered. 'If yes, I think it is accomplished now.' She felt proud. It'd been a while since she had felt that way.

***

'Hey Helen, how was your day?' said Conny as she entered the apartment.

'It was actually very good. Thank you.' Helen smiled back at her sister.

'You look very positive,' Conny commented.

'Yes, I visited our old house and got a great idea for how to solve my problem. What about you, Sis? All good?' Helen asked.

'Yeah, no real problems. I chatted to Mary today about our options. And it seems like we have some plans. So what about your idea?' Conny asked.

'Well, so it is related to this girl at my school. You are much …' suddenly she was interrupted by a phone call. 'Simone, I wonder why she is calling so late.' Helen looked at her phone.

'Hi Simone, what's the story?' Helen asked.

'Hey Helen, listen, I'm on my way to JFK with Francis. We'll be there in three hours. Would you have any space in your apartment for us to spend the night?' Simone asked.

'Of course, Sis! Come on over. What about Marcus?' Helen was surprised but she felt that he might be the cause of that decision.

'I think it is over. We'll chat when I get there. Talk to you soon. Thanks for saving my life,' shouted Simone.

'Any time, Sis, anytime.' Helen was curious what had happened, but at the same time she was happy to have her sister back and to meet her nephew, as well.

'Is she ok?' Conny asked.

'It seems complicated. She is on her way to us from Boston, with Francis,' Helen said.

'Wow. Another interesting story, I guess. The Murphy sisters' lives are definitely not boring,' Conny said with a smile.

'Oh yeah. There is always something crazy happening,' Helen paused for a second. 'So going back to my idea. I need your help. You are very into this topic now, and I hope you can chat to Jane.'

'Wow. Not sure if I'm ready for this,' Conny replied. She seemed to be afraid.

'Yes, you are. You did some research. You heard my story, and probably many more stories. You are ready!' Helen tried to give Conny some confidence.

'Ok. If you say so.' Conny still seemed unconvinced, but really wanted to help Helen to thank her for everything she had done for her.

'Put your shoes on, Jane is in the coffee shop across the road!' Helen said and started putting her shoes on.

'Oh, now … already. Wait … what if I say no?' Conny asked.

'Yeah, "no" wasn't on the table, so … you know.' Helen winked. They went downstairs and crossed the street. They saw her through the window. She was already sitting at a table and sipping some fancy coffee.

'Hi Jane,' Helen started. 'This is my sister Constance.' Conny leaned forward and shook her hand.

'Howya!' Conny tried to play the role of a teenager.

'Hello, nice to meet you Constance,' Jane responded, surprised.

'We wanted to chat with you about your situation,' Helen said.

'Does she know?' Jane asked and looked at Conny.

'Yes,' Helen responded.

'Seriously, Miss Murphy? Do you need to spread the news so quickly?' Jane sounded frustrated.

'Are you kidding me?' Helen could not believe what she was hearing. 'You told the whole class about my secret! That was not easy for me,' Helen continued.

'Secret? You didn't tell me that it was a secret.' Jane looked surprised.

'I told you that my story was a secret. Unbelievable.' Helen was shaking her head. 'Doesn't matter now. Conny knows, and she is here to help you. She is an expert in this kind of situation, she researched a lot on this topic recently.' Helen smiled, looking at Constance.

'Wow. Big words, Sis. I don't really feel like an expert but I will give it a try,' Conny replied.

'Go for it,' Helen encouraged her.

'Did you have any thoughts on how you would like to proceed?' Conny asked Jane.

'Yes. I can't have a baby. I would be alone, because my parents will not help me at all.' Jane was clearly upset about the whole situation.

'What about you? What would you like to do for yourself? I mean, if there weren't going to be any issues with your parents or partner, what would you do? What choice would you make?' Conny was trying to grasp Jane's true feelings.

'If I knew that I would get some support, I would have the baby,' Jane responded.

'Let me tell you a few things I learned recently about abortion,' Conny started saying.

'What do you do for a living?' Jane interrupted.

'I'm working on a project related to abortion.' Conny paused for a moment, looking at Jane. 'I could swear that I have seen your face somewhere.'

'I don't think we have met,' Jane responded confidently.

'Let me continue, then,' Constance resumed. 'Abortion is not an easy topic to chat about. It touches human lives, suffering, problems, it touches the people closest to us. We care about their health and about them living a good life. I won't be telling you horrible stories of people who went through this and decided to abort their babies. But one thing I will tell you: it doesn't work that way, that you abort your baby and the problem is gone. There is something mystical about women conceiving a baby, being pregnant and then giving birth. The bond between a mother and child is there from the very beginning. And as hurtful as this might sound, it doesn't matter how the baby was conceived. Miss Murphy already told you about her experiences. Does she regret what she did? Every day. Why?' Tears began to run down Helen's cheeks very quickly.

'You were pregnant and had an abortion?!' Jane was shocked.

'Oh, yeah. You didn't know about this part. Sorry, Sis,' she looked at Helen's face, feeling guilty. But Helen didn't care anymore. She was an open book.

'Because with the baby, she removed a part of herself,' Conny continued. 'And it is not true that we only fight for the unborn. No, your life matters as well. Or maybe, in different words. Your life and your baby's life matter equally. Your baby doesn't have much to say, so you have to make the call for her or him. But your life is important, and we would like to help you. To support you. Because the baby is not a problem, the problem is your fear of having a baby and everything that will happen after that.'

Jane was looking at Conny very attentively. Helen was happy to see her sister talking about this important topic with this kind of intelligence and passion. She thought about how Conny had really thought this through.

'We don't want to convince you to do anything. We want you to be really free in your decision. You are young, you do not feel fully independent. But when you hear all of those voices saying you should abort your baby because it is your body, and you should be independent – that's not reality. The reality is that women fear for the future of their baby, and their own future, and decide to have an abortion.'

'Don't let the fear control you!' Helen added.

'I think it is late now. I forgot my phone and my dad has just gotten into town,' Jane said.

'Oh, where did he come from? Does he not live with you?' Helen asked.

'No, he works in Geneva. Doing some pro-life stuff or something, I don't know, really,' Jane stood up. 'Thank you for this conversation.'

'You're welcome!' Helen responded.

'And apologies for releasing your secret, Miss Murphy.' Jane bowed her head and left the coffee shop.

'Yeah … no worries, I guess,' Helen responded quietly.

'This is why her face was familiar to me.' Conny was confused and excited at the same time.
'Is she really the daughter of this pro-life guy you were talking with in Geneva? Wow, that's big.' Helen smiled. 'Let's go back to the apartment. I need to make the beds for Simone and Francis.'

***

Simone got to Helen's apartment at around 11 p.m. She was tired, but still emotional. So the three of them chatted until 2 a.m. Francis was so sleepy that he barely said hello to his aunties and fell asleep on the couch.

'In a weird way I feel happy now,' said Simone, lying in bed.

'You are free, Sis, freedom gives us happiness. Sleep well. Goodnight,' Helen responded and fell asleep instantly.

7

'Oh crap, I'm late,' Helen shouted and jumped out of bed. 'That's a great start to the week,' she thought while trying to brush her hair and clean her teeth at the same time.

'You good, Sis?' asked Conny in a sleepy voice with her eyes still closed.

'Yes, I just need to hurry up because I'm going to be late,' Helen responded

'Oh … right,' Conny was asleep again.

In just five minutes Helen was downstairs. She grabbed an electric scooter and accelerated to get going faster. She got to school just one minute before the classes started.

'So glad, I'm not late today,' she thought. She had a smile on her face again. The first class wasn't bad, either. The girls were good, they just did their work and didn't cause any trouble. Helen felt positive again.

'Miss Murphy, could you please come to my office?' Suddenly the headmaster called her to his office. It was not really a surprise. She had expected this, considering that she had not been at school for a week.

'Of course, I'm coming,' Helen responded and followed the headmaster.

'I wanted to catch you before class but could not find you,' the headmaster remarked, quick to discover her morning secret.

'Yes, I was rushing this morning. I was almost late,' Helen tried to explain.

'Oh, I see. I'm glad you were just almost late, not late. We don't want to give a bad example to our children at school.' The headmaster was very clear about school policies.

'Obviously. That is well understood'. Helen didn't want to get into that topic with him, as she knew she would lose. It was his kingdom.

'Let's sit,' he said, pointing at the chairs. 'I wanted to ask, how do you feel?' he asked, sitting down as well.

'I'm doing well. Thank you. My sisters are spending time with me, so that helps.' Helen felt really good, knowing that someone cared about her in that way.

'That's great. I received a call this morning from the father of one of the girls who attend this school,' the headmaster said very slowly.

'Ok …' The smile immediately disappeared from Helen's face. Thousands of thoughts were going through her head. But they were easily summarised in one sentence: It had to be the pro-life fellow. Jane's father. 'I'm done' she thought. 'It is always the same in those kinds of situations. You feel straight away that you are in trouble. The only question is how and when. As much as you know that you did nothing wrong, this is a sensitive situation and someone isn't going to be happy with your opinion, so this will backfire, one way or another.'

'Yeah, so he said that you tried to convince one of our students, his daughter, to have an abortion. I understand your previous life experiences but I would prefer you didn't talk with our students about those kinds of things. They have their parents who can speak with them about this.' The headmaster was very calm.

'No, no, no …' Helen started. 'It was not me, really, but my sister, and it was not convincing her to have an abortion but arguing against having one,' Helen tried to explain herself.

'Even worse. I would prefer we didn't share personal information about our students with people outside this school.' His voice was getting louder.

'It was only my sister, she has some experience and knowledge of this,' Helen continued to defend herself.

'Experience with what? Abortion? Your family had some serious problems,' the headmaster stated. This was going in the wrong direction and Helen was not able to stop it.

'Tell me about it,' Helen said quietly to herself.

'What? I couldn't hear you.'

'Apologies. I will not do it again.' Helen didn't want to argue. For her the case was closed anyway. 'Can I go now?' she asked.

'Not yet. This kind of behaviour is not going to be tolerated in this school. And as much as I like you, Miss Murphy, I have no choice. I will have to suspend you!' he stated.

'What? I can't believe that! I didn't do anything wrong.' Helen was furious.

'Miss Murphy, you had better be careful with your words now. We don't want to change this suspension to an immediate termination.' The headmaster was calm and cold.

'Unbelievable. I'm going. Good day.' Helen stood up and walked out through the door, which she slammed loudly behind her. She grabbed her bag from the teachers' room and left the school. She was angry. It seemed like everything had been going in the right direction and then bang, everything was gone again. She felt disappointed. This was one of those moments when you are still angry, but powerless to shout. You want to cry, but you feel that all the tears are already gone. She got home pretty quickly. She didn't even notice anything on her way back home, really, as her thoughts were somewhere else. When she got to the apartment she was thinking about what to say to Conny. She would definitely be sad that she had got her sister into trouble, Helen thought. But Conny was not home. The apartment was empty.

'Hmm ... ok. That's surprising, that Conny is not here. Well, maybe she had something urgent to do,' she said to herself. She dropped her bag in a corner and decided to lie down for a minute. 'Sleep is good for everything,' she thought. She took her shoes off and lay down on her bed, and covered herself with the blue blanket. It was still pretty early in the morning but she fell asleep quickly.

Half an hour later, the doors were opened wide. Conny was back. She was in tears. She didn't notice Helen in her bed or even see Helen's bag, which she almost tripped over. Something bad had happened and it looked like Conny didn't know how to handle it. She sat down on the couch and covered her face with her hands. That was unusual for her. Many years before she had made a conscious decision to never cry. There was enough suffering and crying in her life, and it didn't help her at all to pour it all out through tears. But these tears now were not caused by her personal situation but by her mission. She felt that she had failed completely.

'Conny, is that you?' Helen's sleepy voice echoed in the apartment.

'Jeez, you scared me.' Conny almost jumped off the couch. 'I thought no one was here.'

'Sorry, Sis, you cannot just cry without anyone hearing,' she replied and smiled with her eyes still closed.

'Yeah, sure …' Conny was still weeping. In a way she was happy that she didn't have to be alone in this situation.

'So what happened? Why are you crying?' Helen asked.

'I got a call this morning. Just after you left,' she stopped and started crying again.

'Calm down, Sis, no one ever died from answering a phone call.' Helen stood up from the bed and went to Constance to hug her. Helen was her old self again, forgetting about her troubles and looking after those who needed consolation.

'Yeah, I know. So it was this guy, the pro-life fighter …'

'Oh … I think I know where this is going'. Helen started connecting the dots.

'So he wanted to meet. You know me, I would usually not get up so early in the morning. But he wanted to chat with me. I hoped that he would finally help me with my project … but I was mistaken.' She started weeping again.

'What did he say to you?' Helen was curious.

'He did not say anything, he shouted at me. He screamed that I'm going after his children. Pushing his daughter to have an abortion, that kind of stuff. I could not say a word. He screamed at me and then just left. And I was standing there, shocked. I couldn't believe what had just happened.' She cried more.

'Poor little thing.' Helen hugged her.

'By the way, why are you home so early? I did not expect you to be home so early … it's only 10 a.m.,' Conny asked Helen.

'Yeah, well, I got suspended,' she replied.

'What? How come? For what?' Conny was shocked again.

'Parental intervention. I guess the same individual as in your case.' A bit of sleep had definitely given Helen some distance from the whole situation.

'No way, what are we going to do now?' Conny was a bit confused.

'I don't know. I guess we should try to fix it,' Helen answered.

'But how?' Conny doubted that they could find a solution for this.

'Well. I have plenty of time to think about it now.'
Helen smiled. It seemed that there was a little
positivity in her soul again.

***

It was Mary's turn to visit the old house. It was
incredible in some ways. No one had been in this
house for so long, before they had all met again.
There was some secret power in this place that was
attracting them to it, in a mysterious way. They
wanted to go back there, for no particular reason.
They felt that they were meeting someone there.
Was it a person? The house was empty. No one was
living there, so probably not. They were meeting their
memories, good memories. Their history, and their
parents' history. And that voice … who was it? Mary
thought about it often. She really wanted to uncover
the mystery.

She got there just before lunchtime. She decided to
extend her lunchtime that day. It was such a lovely
day. It was sunny and there was a little breeze
coming from the east. The traffic was not as bad as
she had expected. It seemed like many people
worked from home these days, because they were
trying to be more efficient with their time. Well,
productivity is the key to success, as they say.

She didn't really have a plan for what to do inside
the house. She was surprised by that herself, as she
was someone who usually knew what to do, and had
a very detailed plan for every step. But the power that
had brought her here was something different. It did
not require any questions, or plans. It just flowed.

She sat down on the couch. She took her cell phone out to put it on the table, and it suddenly started ringing. She answered, 'Mary speaking, how can I help you?' She thought that maybe someone from the office was calling.

'Hi, it's Lisa, the UN commissioner,' she introduced herself nicely and calmly.

'Hi Lisa, good to hear from you.' Mary was happy to hear her voice. She hoped that meeting her husband had helped Lisa to understand her perspective.

'Yeah, the resolution has gone through and it was decided by one vote, mine. The new resolution will be released in the next few weeks and governments will be obligated to implement the new law in their countries over the next twelve months. She was still very calm as she said this.

'Wow. I'm surprised. I thought you had some feelings after all.' Mary was a bit shocked and frustrated. This was when her emotions exploded. Over the past few weeks she had tried to keep her emotional side on a leash but this was just too much to handle.

'I don't appreciate your comment. I have feelings. I'm doing this for the whole of humanity. We are living in difficult times, and we need to empower people to make their own decisions about their lives. Goodbye. I hope the case is closed now. I won't let you play this "paralysed husband" game again.' She hung up. Mary felt powerless...

She dropped her phone. She hadn't thought that it would turn out this way. She had really hoped for a better outcome after yesterday. She had thought it was possible to change that lady's mind. She had been so wrong.

'And what now?' she asked herself, staring out the window. She started walking around to release the emotional steam. There was no point in shouting, crying or doing anything. This was not the first time something hadn't gone her way. 'That's just part of life,' she said to herself many times. She knew that this was not the end of the world. She was disappointed, obviously, but for a moment at least it didn't affect her mood. She focused on this old house, and was curious what she might find there.

'There has to be a speaker somewhere, doesn't there?' she asked herself while climbing the stairs to the attic. 'The voice we heard needed to come from someplace,' she thought. She started looking around. She moved the chairs and the couch and then checked under the table. She looked at every inch of the wall and roof. Nothing. She moved some books.

'Here we go!' she shouted. 'This looks like a speaker. An old-school speaker. You can probably only find those in a museum these days,' she laughed to herself.

'Ha! Even easier!' Mary discovered that this was not a wireless speaker, but there was a wire that was not even in the wall. The cable was hidden under some plaster. Mary carefully removed it, slowly so she didn't damage the whole wall. It took her a while, because it was glued to the wall and floor really well. Finally she figured out that the cable actually went into the floor, so it had to end somewhere downstairs. Possibly in one of the bedrooms. She got up quickly and went down the stairs to the floor the bedrooms were on. The only room they had not looked in when they were there last was their parents' bedroom. They had felt that they shouldn't. They had never really entered it without permission when they were kids, so why would they now?

Mary hesitated for a moment. She didn't know what to expect. What if someone was actually living there, she thought, which sounded pretty crazy even in her own mind. She decided to open the door and go in.

No one was there at the time. But it seemed like someone was sleeping there at some point. The bed was not made, it was really messy. 'Interesting,' she said to herself. 'So this place belongs to somebody,' she added out loud. There were no clothes, no other stuff, nothing. Only the bed, which looked like it was being used. There was no dust on the sheets so someone had used them pretty recently. 'That's creepy,' Mary thought. She wanted to leave the room and forgot what she had been looking for. 'Oh yeah, the speaker.' She stopped when she got to the door. She looked at the ceiling. 'Here we go,' she pointed at the corner of the ceiling, just beside the window.

She took a chair and stood on it. And she grabbed the cable to see where it led. It led to a bedside locker. There were plenty of things stored in the locker. None of it looked valuable to her, even from a historical perspective. She couldn't even say if any of it had belonged to her family, to her parents, or if it belonged to someone else, maybe even to the person who had used to live here. She slowly moved some things to other parts of the locker, and some others she put on the desk, which was just beside the king-size bed. 'Here you are!' She smiled. She found the cable, which was coming through the back of the locker. 'Let's see what you are connected to,' she said quietly.

Under some clothes, there was a small machine to which the cable was connected. 'What the heck is this?' she asked herself. Another prehistoric machine. 'Let me find out online, I don't want to break it,' she said to herself. She took out her phone and took a picture. She clicked and got an answer immediately. 'A cassette player?' she said, asking herself what that meant. She quickly had a look at different pages describing this toy that had last been used in the 1990s. Then she took out the cassette that was inside the box and started looking at it. 'Interesting,' she thought. She put it back and pressed play. She could not hear anything, though. After a second she figured out that the speaker was upstairs, so she ran there. It was the same voice, the same message. She sat on the couch and listened again to the whole speech. When it finished she went downstairs again.

'I wonder if there are more recordings here,' she said to herself as she was walking down the stairs and entering the room again. Beside the player, there was a box with a cassette inside. The label on the box said, 'For Mary'.

'Wow. That's incredible. That's me.' Mary was very excited. She put the cassette into the player and pressed play again. And again she ran upstairs so she could listen to this tape.

'Hi Mary. I was confident that you would figure out this thing and that you would listen to this tape.'

'Dad?' Mary asked, but the voice was still talking.

'Not sure what year it is now. I recorded this in 2030. If you are listening to it, it means that I'm not around anymore. Well, in a material, physical way at least. I hope to be with you all spiritually, at least, until the end of your days.' The voice laughed.

'Why did he record this?' Mary asked herself

'I recorded this tape for you because I missed you. Things didn't really work out between us the way I wanted. Your moving out really hurt me, but it doesn't matter. It was time for you to fly away from the family nest into the evil and unpredictable world. I wanted to tell you two things. One–' he paused for a moment. 'I was always, and will be until my death, very proud of you. Very proud to be your father. You are a smart, and beautiful woman. I was always sure that you were capable of achieving great things and you will find out the truth about life and yourself.' He paused again. 'The second thing is …' He paused for longer this time. 'Don't blame yourself for our deaths. You may have had different opinions on some topics than we had, but it was not you. Our death was inevitable. You were a young girl searching for the truth. Sometimes it takes time. But I know that you will find it, or maybe you have already found it. I miss you. Bye.'

That really touched her. She started crying. It felt like this very short recording addressed the very doubts and needs she was carrying in her heart. She laid down her head on the couch and started thinking about all of those things in her past, and what she was dealing with now. There are so many problems, so many more questions that need to be answered. Could she forgive herself? For what she had done to her parents? And to her husband and son? She closed her eyes. She could not keep them open anymore because the tears were flooding her cheeks like crazy. She started to calm down a bit. She felt in her heart that she wasn't alone. Her father had stopped talking but he was still present, spiritually, like he had said. She felt that, in some strange way. She smiled. Some happy thoughts came to her mind. She stopped crying. The pain changed, or it was soothed by some indescribable power. She fell asleep. In a funny way, that three-minute recording had switched her focus to something else. Twenty minutes ago she had been trying to figure out who was sleeping in the bed and who played the cassettes. Now, the only question was: 'what is the truth?'

***

'Hey girls, how is your day going?' said Simone, entering the apartment.

'Yeah, could be better, I guess, but we are trying to stay positive,' Conny responded.

'How do you like New York, Frank?' Helen asked.

'It is nice. A bit too loud, but well, if they have ice cream I should be fine.' He smiled smartly. Helen laughed.

'You are a funny little guy. Of course they have ice cream here. We have some in our freezer as well.' Helen started walking to the kitchen.

'It is really hot outside, 110 degrees at least. These days you cannot survive without air conditioning,' Simone said and grabbed a glass of water.

'How did the house hunting go?' Conny asked.

'It was not bad. Obviously we won't be able to afford to rent an apartment in Manhattan. But Brooklyn, Staten Island, Long Island, those should be options for us.'

'That's great. Happy for you, Sis,' Helen responded.

'So what happened today? You seemed a bit depressed.' Simone sat down.

'Yeah, It was a pretty exciting morning,' Helen said.

'You phrased it nicely, Sis. We were crying like little babies. No offence, Frank, Conny added.

'I'm not a baby. I'm a big boy,' Francis responded.

'Sorry Frank, you are a big boy. That's true. My lovely nephew.' Conny gave him a kiss on his forehead.

'Why were you crying? What happened?' Simone asked Conny.

'Why would you even care?' Conny said unexpectedly. .

Simone ignored that. First Helen and then Conny started telling their stories of their day. Simone was very interested in all the details so it took some time to get through everything. Suddenly Simone's phone rang.

'Hello?' she answered as she was unsure who it was; the phone number was hidden.

'It's me, Marcus,' he started.

'Why are you calling from a hidden phone number?' she asked.

'Not your business! I will be quick. You will not threaten my clients. I don't care what you have heard from Greg's wife or what documents you have. I know that you are incapable of doing anything about it because you are worthless and you have no education or experience with those kinds of things. Also, if you still decide to do something stupid, I will really make your life miserable. Where are you now? Where is Francis?' he asked at the end.

'Not your business!' Simone shouted and hung up. She started crying. She didn't have to say anything to Helen and Conny, they had heard everything. Helen had only covered Francis' ears so he didn't have to listen to his father treating his mother like that.

'Wow. One day. Three sisters crying. I hope Mary had a better day than we did.' She winked at Helen. As much as Conny felt some empathy for her, she still felt inside a reluctance towards Simone. Something that had started in the past, and that could not be easily forgotten.

8

Simone could not sleep. In one way she was terrified. She had never heard Marcus say so many hurtful words. She was disappointed. 'How come I even married him?' It was that feeling when you have known someone for many years and then you discover that person's dark side. And she knew that everyone has a dark side, she had it as well. But for some reason it was just the first time she had actually seen it with her own eyes. And it was scary. How far was Marcus from physically hurting her or Frank? She didn't know, but still, it was something new to her, and she didn't really know what to do with it. Maybe it was her mistake. She really should not have gotten involved in some business she was not familiar with and had zero knowledge about. Marcus was right, she didn't have an education. 'I'm probably dumb,' she thought as she was lying on the bed and looking at the ceiling. And it was strange that Marcus had reacted like that.

She was not sure what had happened there. Maybe there was something that had triggered him. She had not seen him like that before. It was just so awkward. Or maybe it was just her, she hadn't wanted to see him that way. It was a terrifying experience for her, but at the same time she felt safe.

She was miles away from home. There was no chance that he could find her. He had no idea where Helen's apartment was, and he would have no idea where she would be when Simone rented an apartment. Simone worried about Frank, though. At the end of the day she didn't want him to lose his connection with his father.

Conny woke up early. 'You are awake already, nice!' she said to Simone.

'Yeah, I'm actually still trying to fall asleep,' Simone responded.

'Wow, it doesn't seem like it's going to happen in the near future from what I can see,' Conny replied and smiled like nothing had happened last night.

'Yeah, well. What are you up to?' Simone asked.

'New Yorkers wake up early to jog, so I need to wake up even earlier,' she responded.

'I didn't mean that. Why did you say that I don't care about you?' she asked Conny. It seemed like her reaction upset Simone no less than Marcus's awful call had.

'You ignored me for many years,' Conny said, not hiding her feelings but looking directly into her eyes.

'We all did, we are sorry. Life was not easy on us after our parents' death,' Simone tried to defend herself.

'That's another story. I understand that they tried to stand up for what they believed in, but at the same time they hurt us, their children, the most,' she paused for a second. 'You ignored me before as well, I remember I felt like I didn't exist for you.' Her voice started to shake because of the sad memories.

'Hmm' Simone replied, as she didn't really know how to answer. 'I'm sorry, Sis. I was not an easy kid. I needed a lot of attention, and when you showed up in this world, I was just jealous. I think ignoring you was just an act of desperation, a defensive reaction. I'm really sorry.' Simone realised how much this must have hurt Conny, and she knew that it had been wrong.

'What time is it then?' Simone asked, just to change the topic.

'Four in the morning,' Conny replied, winking at Simone.

'You are crazy!' Simone laughed at her.

'Gotta go now, before the New Yorkers wake up. I'm planning to go to the old house later. Do you want to join me?' Conny asked from the door.

'I might. Need to see what to do with Frank,' Simone responded.

Simone finally fell asleep. At 5 a.m. your brain is so tired that there is no chance of not falling asleep, unless you are on drugs. She woke up just three hours later, to find Frank playing with his Auntie Helen.

'Sorry, Sis, didn't want to wake you up. I heard you went to sleep pretty late,' Helen said, smiling. 'You have a lovely boy, Simone, and he really likes airplanes.'

'Yeah, he is crazy about them.' Simone stood up and kissed Frank and Helen. 'Thanks, Helen. I appreciate that. Let me take a quick shower,' she said and disappeared into the bathroom. After a few minutes she came back.

'Not sure what your plans are for today,' she started.

'I'm kind of suspended, so no plans, really,' Helen answered.

'Lovely!' she smiled. 'I don't mean lovely that you are suspended. That's unfair and awful. But …'

'Shoot, Sis. What can I do for you? I have loads of time.' Helen was quick with her response.

'Could you stay with Frank this morning?' she asked

'Mummy, where are you going?' Frank asked.

'I'm going to our old house, if Auntie agrees to stay with you,' Simone looked at Helen.

'Of course I will, it will be a pleasure,' Helen responded.

'Franky, what are we going to do today? Maybe we can go to the zoo?' she asked the little guy.

'The zoo! Yeah … what is a zoo?' he looked confused.

'It is a place where you can see animals that usually live in the wilderness. Well, these days they mostly live in zoos, unfortunately …'   Simone said.

'Yeah, it's a shame we killed so much wildlife. Our planet is in a really bad shape. When I was studying I was in a group related to saving the environment, etc. I need to tell you some stories about that, it was very interesting to learn what the earth looked like when our parents were children,' Helen added.

'Yeah, definitely. It would be good to hear about the good old times. I don't want to rush off on you, but if possible, I would like to leave now,' Simone said.

'Of course. Go. Maybe you can still avoid the traffic,' Helen responded.

'That would be nice. Thank you very much, Sis. I really need some space now, just for a few hours to catch my breath after that mess.' Simone gave her a kiss on the cheek.

'Love you so much my little hero.' Simone hugged and kissed Frank. 'I will be back soon. Enjoy the zoo!' she shouted and left the apartment.

***

Mary jumped out of bed. 'Yikes, I can't be late for this. This is my last chance,' she said out loud to encourage herself to speed up. She had come home pretty late the night before. She had actually fallen asleep in the old house. When she woke it was already dark outside. She rushed home, but she was feeling better. She wasn't sure if it was just sleep or if maybe the whole house had made her feel better, and that crazy feeling that maybe there was someone still living there.

Her husband and son were still asleep. She took the car and drove to the airport. It was raining heavily. In fact it was pouring like they hadn't seen in New York in years. The roads were almost flooded. It was funny to think that with all the advances in technology in this world, no one had really ever thought about as small an issue as rainwater. Maybe it could be reused or something. There were tonnes of water coming down, and some regions in the world had no water at all, she thought to herself while driving in those difficult weather conditions.

When she got to the airport it was late already. She hoped that the flight would be delayed, or maybe the commissioner would be late getting to the airport. And she was right. She parked her car and ran into the terminal. She looked at the list of departing flights, and saw that the Geneva flight was delayed, along with the others. 'I guess the weather did its job,' she said to herself while looking at the departure screen.

It was one thing to get to the airport, another to find that lady from the UN. Maybe she had already gone through security, maybe not. This was really her last chance. She quickly moved to the security gates, as this was the only place in this huge terminal where she was actually a hundred percent certain that the woman had to pass through. Mary also quickly checked the UN's social media to see if there were any meetings today, and she found one. There was a morning meeting for all UN commissioners. And it had finished just twenty minutes ago. That would mean that even if she had a very fast car, she would never have got to the airport so quickly, not in New York, and not in that weather.

She stood just beside the security gate for diplomats. It would be much easier to find her here than a regular person. Not too many diplomats went through those gates. And she was lucky. Ten minutes later, the commissioner and her assistant showed up at the door of the terminal. For a minute Mary thought about how to approach her because she was afraid that the commissioner's assistant wouldn't let her get close. Again, she was lucky, for some reason her assistant just disappeared and the commissioner was left on her own and she was walking in Mary's direction. She was looking at her mobile the whole time, so she had not noticed Mary, who had been watching. Mary decided to approach her and say what she wanted to say.

'Hello, it is me again,' Mary quickly reintroduced herself.

'You again?' the commissioner quickly looked at her.

'Yes, sorry for bothering you …' Mary began slowly and kindly.

'You are not bothering me, because I'm not planning to stop. I have a flight to catch,' she replied and started walking towards the security gate.

'Wait!' Mary shouted. 'You need to listen to me. It is very important.' Mary tried to stop her.

'Ok. You have exactly three minutes.' The commissioner looked at her watch.

'Ok. Let me start with this. It was never my intention to use my family to convince you to change your mind and consider my ideas,' Mary said.

'Good to know. I accept your apology,' the commissioner responded.

'Really?' Mary thought that she was secretly laughing at her. 'I really believe that life itself is more important than quality of life. I really believe – and in a way I have experienced this as well – that people whose quality of life is far from ideal are still very happy and satisfied with their lives. Life is about love and when those people feel loved they want to live their lives for as long as possible. I'm sure that it is the same with your lover in Switzerland.' The commissioner looked around to check that no one had heard what Mary had said.

'Your decision, your declaration, will change the world. Societies and governments will use that power to control people and make them do things that they will regret for the rest of their lives,' Mary added.

The commissioner looked a bit more understanding than she had the last time; she was looking into Mary's eyes and she even smiled at her, briefly. She touched her shoulder and turned around to go to the security gates. She didn't say a word.

'What does your smile mean?!' Mary shouted at her, but she only turned around and smiled at her again.

'That's confusing. No idea what she was thinking … maybe she was ok with my idea,' she thought to herself. It was not raining anymore. Mary returned to the car park and drove home. In a way she felt proud of what she had done. She had finally had the courage to say the things that were coming from her heart. When she got home she discovered that her husband was not asleep anymore. She looked into his eyes and she knew that what she had said to the commissioner was the truth. He felt loved by her despite all their history, and she was important to him not only because she was helping him to live but because he always remembered when he had first fallen in love with her. There was this bond between them, a true love that was bigger than their lives, than their capabilities, than themselves. They were a family, and they had a son they wanted to raise together. She smiled, and she knew that her smile meant a lot to Eugene. Maybe it was even a life-giving lifebuoy.

***

Simone decided to get an underground train. She knew that with this weather, the traffic would be so terrible that she would need half a day to get to Long Island. She really wanted to visit the house again. She felt that she wanted more than just that first visit. Her mind had been somewhere else at the time. But things had changed for her and for her sisters since that April weekend.

Not being with Frank, not having to drive, was good for her. She was able to start thinking about her life. What had it been like when she was a child? And who was she really? She was asking herself these questions while she sat on the busy underground train. Fortunately enough when she got off the train and had to walk through the park it was not raining anymore. Some parts of the park were flooded but besides that everything was all right. And she was not wet. She had never liked to carry rainproof jackets or umbrellas with her. But at the same time she hoped that she wouldn't get soaking wet.

She found the keys under the doormat. She smiled when she saw them. It was actually her parents' idea. No magic apps that can open and close everything for you. Just an old, rusty set of keys. She opened the door. The first thing she did was go to the fridge to see if there was anything in it. She had this habit of checking the fridge when she was at home, not because she was hungry but because she had to always make sure that Marcus's favourite foods were in the fridge. 'I hope he will have something to eat while I'm away,' she thought. 'Why am I even thinking about this. What is wrong with me?' Obviously there was nothing in the fridge. Even if there had been something, Helen would have cleaned it out the last time they had been there.

She went upstairs and visited her room first. She sat down on the bed. 'This room looks so small,' she said quietly. She rested her head on the dusty pillow. 'I remember how difficult it was for me to fall asleep here,' she thought. I wanted Mum to stay with me, and Dad afterwards. I remember him telling me that I was beautiful, and smart, and that I was capable of doing anything I wanted. But am I?' She started to cry a little. 'I don't really remember other men besides Dad saying that. Even Marcus ...he never told me that I was beautiful, or smart.'   As she thought about this, more tears ran down her cheeks. 'Maybe dad was wrong,' she sobbed. 'I'm not beautiful at all. No one really cares about me. Maybe Frank will be different. He will love me,' Simone continued, talking to herself.

   She got up and walked up the stairs to the attic. She sat down on the chair and grabbed a book that was lying just beside the chair, on the table. 'Wow, I have not read a proper paper book for ages, probably since school,' she thought to herself. She opened it to a folded-over page, and started reading somewhere in the middle of the page, where some text had been highlighted.

'I have created you, says the Lord.' She started reading. 'This is why you are the most precious person I created. You are the most beautiful, because love itself, God, created you. This is what I'm telling you and no one can change a word of what I have said. Because you are in me, and I am in you.' She stopped reading.

'Interesting,' she said to herself and started staring out the window. She didn't really have many more thoughts on this. She was just sitting and watching, and listening to the silence. The words that she had read kept coming back to her, over and over. They were very firm, and at the same time they were sensitive and touched her heart. She listened to them again and again, trying to analyse everything.

Suddenly someone started knocking on the door. 'Simone, you there?' someone shouted. I can't open the door.'

'The door, right,' Simone quickly woke from that moment of contemplative meditation. She ran down the stairs, grabbed the keys that she had left on the kitchen table and opened the door.

'Hi Simone,' Conny said when the door opened. 'How are you doing?' Conny asked, when she saw Simone's red eyes and wet cheeks.

'Doing well. Thanks. Just remembering some sad memories, and …yeah,' she replied and Conny passed her and sat down on the couch.

'I'm really tired after my jog this morning, the weather was not pleasant at all,' Conny said.

'Yeah, I can imagine. Half of the city was flooded, I heard on the news.'

'That sounds accurate. When I came back to the apartment, I was soaking wet. Had to change all my clothes,' Conny exclaimed.

'I hope Helen and Frank are doing fine?' Simone asked but she wasn't really speaking to Conny.

'I didn't see them at the apartment,' Conny responded

'They went to the zoo. Hopefully they are fine,' Simone said. 'Tell me, Conny, how are you? How is your mission going?' she asked.

'Hmm … Not sure what to say,' Conny responded, feeling a bit ashamed.

'You ok?' Simone asked.

'Yeah, it is just a bit weird. You've never asked me about my stuff,' Conny responded frankly.

'Oh, I have never thought about that.' Simone looked a bit confused.

'Yeah, I don't think we had a good relationship when we lived at home. Or maybe there was no relationship at all,' Conny continued.

'Maybe … I think I know where you are going with this, but please continue,' Simone said.

'I don't want to hurt you, but you were not the best sister to me …' Conny responded, coming back to the conversation they had had not so long before.

'Nothing can hurt me more than what I have heard from my husband. And I would agree, I probably was not the best sister. I recently had some time to work through some things,' Simone said.

'Yeah. I am the youngest and I didn't really know Mary, as she moved out of home before I was aware of what was going on. I was not too mature, either, when our parents passed away. You were probably the closest to me because we're closest in age. But it seems like Helen was closer to me, or at least she tried the most.' Conny was touched by her words.

'Yeah, Helen was always great. A real family person. Always there, waiting to help,' Simone agreed with her.

'And you didn't see me, you ignored me so many times. Even when we met again a few weeks ago, I felt you were cold towards me. You weren't excited to see me, you were not happy. Like you had no idea who I was. That really ruined that reunion, you know?' Conny started crying.

'I don't know what to say, sister,' Simone responded as she hugged her. 'I know that I was cold, I have many problems myself and it was difficult to move on from all of that. As I said before, I was the youngest for so long, I was the most important in our family. All the attention was on me, and then you showed up. I think this was my defensive reaction. I lost Mum and Dad's attention, and you took my place. I was a little kid then, but I think that somewhere inside I decided to ignore you because I was mad.' Simone looked into Conny's eyes.

'That probably explains that ...' Conny added.

'I'm really sorry Constance. Please forgive me? Let's restart this relationship.' Simone hugged her again and sobbed quietly.

'I do forgive you, Sis. I love you no matter what. I want to be a part of your life, and want you to be a part of my life. I think this is what I was missing for all of those years.' Conny hugged her back.

***

Simone returned to the apartment just after lunchtime. Conny had to finish some stuff on the way back, so they split up. Helen came home with Frank just a few minutes after Simone.

'How was it, Franky?' Simone asked.

'It was great, Mum. I saw some very big animals. Then Auntie took me to the place where you can see snakes and spiders. It was so cool.' Frank sounded very excited.

'Your auntie is very cool!' Simone looked at Helen. 'Thank you Sis, Franky had a lot of fun, it seems.' Simone kissed her cheek.

'Yeah, I hope so. He is a very good boy. What time is it?' she asked

'Half past one,' Simone answered.

'I have to go, I meant to go to the school for a moment. And soon school will be over and the teachers will be gone five minutes after the kids are gone,' she laughed.

'Good luck, Sis,' Simone said.

Helen left the apartment. The weather was much better than in the morning. Finally the sun had come out from behind the dark, puffy clouds and was shining like it should in June. 'What a lovely weather to have a difficult discussion at school with the headmaster,' Helen laughed to herself. The last lessons hadn't quite finished when she got to the school. 'Good,' she thought. The worst thing that could have happened would have been to see all the teachers and students leaving the premises. She went directly to the hall that led to the headmaster's office. She knocked on the door.

'Please come in,' a male voice called from inside. Helen opened a door and entered the room.

'Good afternoon, Sir!' She smiled.

'Oh, it's you. Miss Murphy, how can I help you?' he asked.

'I don't think I had a fair chance to say something about my case. So I would like you to listen to what I have to say.' Helen tried to be very serious and strong.

'I'm listening,' the headmaster responded quickly.

'My personal history is very hurtful for me. It was not my idea to live a life like this. I was put into a difficult situation and had to make a decision. Would I make the same decision now? Probably not. I'm in a different state of mind. I look at life through a different lens now. That doesn't mean, though, that it is not painful. I still suffer from the consequences of my decisions. When the girl from my class came to me with her problem, I was momentarily taken back to the situation I was in years ago. I was terrified. I felt straight away what this teenage girl was feeling. When similar things happened to me, I was older than she is now.'

'Where are you going with this, Miss Murphy? I don't have all day.' The headmaster didn't look very touched.

'Well, ok …let me speed this up for you. What I wanted to say is that it was not my intention or my sister's intention to do anything hurtful to Jane. She is a lovely girl, and we wanted her to make a decision. The best possible one for her and her baby.'

'Yeah, whatever. Are you finished?' the headmaster said

'I'm done. I can see it is pointless to talk to you and explain myself.' Helen was a bit upset.

'Goodbye Ms Murphy,' he said and started looking at his notepad.

'Yeah, whatever. Thank you for your time,' Helen said and rushed out the door. When she got outside she saw Jane.

'Ms Murphy, where have you been?' she asked.

'I've been suspended,' Helen answered quickly.

'What? How come?' Jane was surprised.

'Oh, so you didn't know. How are you feeling?' Helen asked.

'Well ...' suddenly an older man came running over.

'Leave her alone! She doesn't need any more of your advice,' he shouted

'Dad, stop!' Jane cried and ran to get into the car.

'Oh, so you are the powerful dad,' Helen said calmly.

'Yes, I am. Do you want to see how powerful I can be?' he asked and got back into the car.

'Sure, bring it on,' said Helen, quietly hoping he would not hear her.

***

That evening when they had all gathered in Helen's apartment, Conny stood up unexpectedly and started talking: 'It was a rough day for all of us. We have cried, we are sad because it did not work out the way we anticipated. We are not the only one's suffering in this world, in one way or another. This is a part of our life. I know how we were raised and I know that religious thinking is not popular in this rational world. But I wanted to share some thoughts with you that might surprise you. I feel that this is the right moment for them.

'For a long time I couldn't understand why the loving God is letting his people suffer. Christians were always linking this to the Way of the Cross, and Jesus' last hours in this world. But I just couldn't get this.

'God doesn't want us to suffer. He wants our happiness, he wants our health. But at the same time, he asks us about the cross, asks us to take it, and carry it through our whole life. So what could it be, then? Something that is always there, that makes us suffer but doesn't really depress us, or that shouldn't, really. A while ago I discovered that, I think. The truth is that we are the cross. It comes from our deepest existence. We are not the people God wanted us to be, before Original Sin. We are people who want to do good, but we feel limited. We want to love others but we can't do it easily. We can always see that there is something in us that is not perfect. Even if the world tells us that it is normal, and that this is the way we were born, there is this voice in our hearts and souls that says: "No, there is more, because you were made in the image of God".

'Accepting a cross in this scenario means two things, I believe. One, that we want to discover who the "real me" is, and be honest, that cross will probably get heavier over time. The second thing, which is even more important, is that we need to accept that we cannot carry that cross on our own. We need Christ to help us. Even He needed help because he was human and weak.

'This cross will not go away. You will not wake up one day and realise that the disease is gone, and you are healthy again. Or that you are free from sin. No. Life will bring you more situations where you will be tested and your reaction to them will be your cross. It is not a disease or a sin that is our cross, it is our response to it.

We are not able to see the full picture of every circumstance we are in and every suffering. The cross is there independently of whether we accept something or not. When you independently choose the cross, you choose love.'

Simone's sisters listened to her and were amazed, because they hadn't expected those powerful words from their youngest sister. They didn't know how to respond to this speech, which definitely came from the deepest places of Conny's heart. Conny sat down and they stayed quiet for a little while.

9

'Good morning Helen,' a female voice said in the almost empty apartment.

'What?' Helen responded sleepily.

'It is 9 a.m., Helen. Your calendar for this morning and afternoon is free. The weather is sunny, ninety-one degrees. As you have not been going to the gym recently, I would recommend going for a jog. Your weight has gone up in the last five days. I would suggest having porridge with fruit for breakfast instead of a full English breakfast.' The voice was very convincing.

'Oh … give me a break today, will ya? I really need to remove some data input for this assistant, she is getting too annoying,' Helen said to herself quietly. She got up and went to the bathroom. After cleaning her face she went to take a quick, hot shower. The shower suddenly stopped.

'What the heck?' Helen said loudly. 'Carrie, what is happening with the water?' she asked the assistant.

'There will be an outage today between 9.10 a.m. and 11.30 a.m., due to limited resources. Do you want to hear more about why water is limited? There is a great podcast on this topic. Do you want me to play it?' the female voice asked.

'No, thank you. I will skip it this time. Everyone knows why we have limited water supplies, because we are slowly killing the earth. I'm glad I don't have any shampoo in my hair anymore.' Helen left the bathroom. She put some clothes on and went to the kitchen to prepare breakfast. The coffee had already been prepared for her and was waiting in the coffee machine.

'Thank you, Carrie, lovely coffee as always!' she said.

'You are welcome,' the assistant responded. Helen searched for some food and said, 'There is no bacon …or eggs, either. Carrie, I thought your suggestions were based on health recommendations,' she said.

'Yes, but research shows that most human beings still choose unhealthy foods, ignoring health recommendations,' the voice responded

'So you are more realistic, and also make suggestions based on the availability of products. You are a smart beast!' Helen praised her.

'Yes, that's based on another study that was conducted in the twentieth century: people eat whatever is available in their fridge for breakfast, instead of going to the shop for their favourite food before eating anything,' the voice said.

'Yep, we are lazy. We will have to buy bacon and eggs so we can restock the fridge,' Helen said.

'Not necessary, let me take care of that,' Carrie responded.

'Oh you cheeky monkey, so you are hiding the tasty stuff,' Helen started laughing.

'As I said, those foods are not available at the moment and I recommend eating porridge.' Carrie laughed.

'You laughed. That's unbelievable!' Helen smiled.

'Yeah, that's our new feature.' Carrie laughed again.

'Fair enough, I will have some fruit … and porridge.' Helen put everything in a bowl.

'The assistant was very useful to Helen. And not only in the sense that it turned on the coffee machine; when Helen was lonely, she chatted with Carrie to cheer herself up. As with everything, there were pros and cons to these kinds of helpful machines. They knew a lot about you, to be as useful as possible in your day-to-day life. That unfortunately meant that the machine was also making decisions for you. And the human ability to make any decisions in life was decreasing. We can argue about whether eating porridge or bacon is a decision we want to make or if we can just outsource it, but do we not want to make those bad decisions sometimes? Making right decisions all the time is just boring, and no fun whatsoever. This seemed to be a common issue nowadays. People became dependent on these machines, so that they couldn't make any decisions before asking the assistant first. They were like children, not willing to make a call, or take any responsibility.

'School is calling, do you want me to answer?' Carrie asked.

'Sure … I did not expect this. Let me sit down,' Helen said, and sat down on the couch.

'Good Morning Miss Murphy. Headmaster Wilkovitz here. I just wanted to let you know about a recent decision that was made by the teachers' and parents' association meeting last night. The commission decided to terminate our contract with you. Your services are not required anymore. To avoid causing a disturbance or confusion, please do not visit school to collect your belongings. We will courier them back to you in the next few days. Goodbye and I wish you all the best in your future career.' The headmaster hung up. Helen didn't say a word. She hadn't even said 'hi' or 'bye'. She was quiet. Her face changed. She went from laughing and smiling as she had been during her conversation with Carrie, to not smiling and having tears in her eyes. She covered her eyes with her hands, like she wanted to stop crying, or hide so no one could see her.

'What am I going to do?' she asked herself out loud. 'This will go onto my record, I will never find a job as a teacher, ever again. My future definitely won't be in teaching. I love that job so much … oh … why, why, why?' she shouted at herself.

'Do you want me to play some music that will cheer you up?' Carrie asked.

'Yeah, whatever,' she responded with no enthusiasm. The music started playing. It was cheerful, but not enough to cheer Helen up. She ate some fruit and left the porridge. She was not hungry anymore.

'I have to go for a walk,' she said and put on her runners. 'Stop the music, Carrie. I'm going out,' she said and slammed the door.

'Ok. The music has been stopped now. Enjoy your walk,' Carrie responded. The weather was really nice. There were almost no clouds. A perfect day for a jog or just a walk. Helen was not really in the mood for a jog, or even for a walk but she felt that she could not just stay in her apartment and do nothing. It would not really do her any good. She could eat some unhealthy food, drink some unhealthy drinks, even alcohol. No, she didn't want to depress herself more. It is always easier to do nothing, lie on the couch and fill your stomach with sweets, but it would not help her in the long run. And she knew that, that was why she had decided to go out. To get some fresh air, as fresh as it can be in a city like New York. She also wanted to focus on other things, not only herself. When you walk, you need to pay attention to your surroundings. You don't want to be hit by a mad driver or mugged by some random, less fortunate New Yorker.

She was already outside, she was passing people on the street. Some faces were familiar; neighbours, people in the shops or even beggars. Not thinking about her current situation was healthy for her, and she started to slowly heal. Her thoughts were going in different directions. She started to notice some changes in her neighbourhood. Some stores were gone, some new places had opened up. It was refreshing. So many things were happening around her, and she finally started noticing. People's lives were changing the same way her life had started to change now. Suddenly she saw a small old building between two skyscrapers.

'Wow, that is pretty amazing. A small old building between all those huge skyscrapers,' she said to herself. 'What is that? I think I remember this place,' she thought. She went a little closer and read the plaque outside: 'St Faustina Catholic Church', it read.

'I remember this place. This is where Mum and Dad used to bring us for Mass every Sunday. I'm surprised it is still here,' she thought. She decided to look inside. Wondering if it was even open, she approached the old wooden door. She pushed it and it made a very unpleasant, squeaky sound. 'Oh, wow. That was loud, lucky we are in the loudest city in the world,' she said quietly. Inside the church was made almost entirely of wood. There were very old mosaics on the walls. The inside looked neglected, there was dust everywhere, it looked like it was not really used anymore. The church was not too large, so she was at the first bench in just seconds.

'It has definitely changed since the last time I was here.' Helen sat down on the bench after quickly wiping inches of dust from it. She tried to recall some memories from her visits to that church. She remembered Mum singing and Dad sometimes reading scripture. Without being aware of it she knelt down.

'God, what should I do now?' she shouted, like an inside voice had just blown up. 'I really messed this up. I had a great job, I liked that job. I changed all of this because of some weird mission and a letter from someone, my dead father maybe, or some stranger. Who knows. I wasted my opportunity. Everything will go into my file and I'll be done as a teacher.' Her head started spinning, she could not believe what she had done. Her choices were so illogical, she realised.

'Why? Why? Why? I'm so stupid,' she shouted. 'Dad, why did you involve me in all of this? Why? I messed up this mission, Jane's life, and my life. What was the purpose of it all?' She closed her eyes, and spent a few minutes just sitting in silence. She didn't want to talk to anybody. She was tired. She just wanted to be alone. After twenty minutes she got up and started coughing. 'That dust is killing me,' she said. She started walking back towards the door. 'Jeez!' she shouted. 'Who are you? Are you ok?' She had suddenly seen a monk kneeling in the corner of the church.

'Did you hear what I was saying? she asked him. His head was hidden by his hood, and he was looking at the ground. He didn't respond immediately. 'That's a bit creepy,' Helen said. 'I hope you are not dead or something.' When she still didn't get a response she started walking back towards the exit.

'I'm not dead. I'm just listening to what God has to say to me. You should try it sometime as well,' he answered and hid his head in the hood again.

'Ok. I'm not sure what that means, but fine,' Helen responded while still walking towards the exit. She left the church. Rush hour was over but traffic in New York City is always the same. She walked for another hour or two, not saying much, not even thinking much. She was watching the people around her and listening, hoping that maybe some of the words she heard would be coming directly from God.

***

Conny got back to the apartment at around 10 a.m. 'What a beautiful weather for jogging outside,' she said. She got something to drink, took off her runners and lay down on the couch. 'Let's see what is happening on social media. Let's see how hate and love are triggering people to have big fights over things that don't really affect them directly.'

While she was lying there the doorbell rang. Conny got up and opened the door.

'Hello,' said a courier. 'I have a letter for Miss Constance Murphy.'

'That's me, thank you.' Conny took the letter from the courier.

'You are welcome. Could you please just sign here?' he asked and she did it with her own cell phone.

'Of course.' Conny signed. 'Goodbye,' she said and closed the door.

'What is this?' she asked herself and started opening the envelope. She sat down on the couch and took a letter out of the envelope. She started to read.

Dear Miss Murphy, we would like to inform you that we have been called …

She stopped reading. Her expression was surprised and terrified at the same time.

'What the heck?' she shouted when she finished reading it. 'I can't believe that.' She started reading it again.

'I'm in the shit now, in *big* trouble,' she said out loud and stopped reading again. What am I going to do now? I will go to prison. Stupid missions, stupid letters,' she sat down again, this time on the chair in the kitchen. She took her cell phone out and started texting. She messaged all her sisters, but didn't get a quick reply from anyone. She decided to leave the house as well, like Helen. She just could not sit at home now. She needed to refresh her mind and thoughts. She decided to go back to her parents' old house, hoping maybe there would be something there that would change her focus.

She took the car and it drove her to the old house. She entered; no one else was there. She found the key under the doormat this time. She went directly upstairs, first to her own old room. She sat down on her bed and looked around. 'Where did I leave that letter?' she asked herself. After looking around for a minute, she found it lying right beside the bed. She started reading it again. As if she could have missed something there. Or maybe there was some more text on the other side, or maybe just a simple 'just kidding' … but no … there was nothing. She dropped the letter and hid her face behind her hands and started sobbing.

'There is nothing left, no hope. I'm done. They will definitely put me in prison, I already have a history of breaking the law, they will see that … I'm really done!' she shouted, crying. She went to the attic because there was nothing to do in the bedroom. She thought that maybe she would discover something there that would consume her attention so she would not have to think about this situation.

In the attic she sat down on the chair and looked around. At first she got a bit angry and upset. She just had to let it all out of her heart. 'Why did you leave us? You left us in this freaking crazy world! With no one to take care of us. I really hate you for that,' she shouted through tears. 'What kind of parents leave their 13-year-old child in this evil world? Why would you do that?!' she cried. After a few minutes she calmed down. 'I needed that,' she said calmly, smiling faintly.

'Dad, is this the place where you found yourself?' she asked loudly. There was no response but she knew that this was the truth. Her dad had spent a portion of every day in this attic office space, a little, independent country of his own. Away from this world and its madness. Maybe she had never understood this, or in some way had wanted her Dad to be more present in her life, but it was probably hard for him to live in this world where almost everyone was against him and his beliefs. She was trying to understand her parents' reasons for leaving.

'But for some reason you came to this place and found the strength to live your life,' she said. 'Maybe I can find some strength here as well,' she added. 'Who am I, really? What is the purpose of my life?' she asked herself. It would be great if you could walk me through this … Mum, Dad …' she added. In a way that mission was difficult, but not because of the subject. 'I guess I should have figured this out a long time ago, that those pro-life and pro-choice folks don't really want to have anything to do with women choice and abortion problem. They are just happy to shout about it, shout at the other side and accept the status quo. It was difficult because of me. Maybe this is what the mission was all about. To address my own problems,' she thought.

Conny spent some time there. She needed to. Everyone needs that sometimes: to be alone, to find their own identity. To find themselves. In this busy, hectic and crazy world we have no time to stop and think about what is really important. And our personal mental health is important. She found some calmness in her heart, read some encouraging messages from her sisters and decided to go back to the apartment. In a few days she would have to face all of her problems, but before she had to do that, she could still spend time with her sisters, who were there to support her from now on.

***

This was not the end of the drama for the Murphy sisters that day. Simone had also received a letter. She was not even in the apartment at the time, it happened somewhere on the stairs. A lost courier who didn't have an apartment number on the letter tried to find someone who could direct him. Simone was passing with Frank and he asked her. Surprisingly, he got lucky, she was the intended recipient. But this was not a good message for Simone. She was happy that Frank couldn't read properly yet. It was not a happy birthday card, with unicorns or balloons. It was a letter from the courts informing her that her husband had filed for custody of Frank. She suddenly realised that she could lose the most important thing in her life: Frank. Frank saw that his mum had started crying and asked: 'Is everything okay, Mummy?' Simone stopped sobbing for a moment and hugged him.

'Yes son, we will be fine, don't worry,' she responded. It was difficult to tell if she really meant it. She looked terrified and sad. She thought for a little while, and when Frank went to play with his toys, she decided to call Marcus. She put some notes together on what she wanted to say to him. Frank was the most important person in the whole world to her, she could not just leave him. She knew that Marcus was a great lawyer, she had no chance against him. So she decided to swallow her pride and just apologise and promise not to get involved in that technology company's case anymore. She thought that maybe appealing to him would touch his heart. It didn't. Marcus did not even pick up her call. She wasn't sure why. Maybe he was just busy, but Simone tried a few more times later the same day and it was the same. She started losing hope. She was mad at herself. She has had a good, easy life. Then this mission had happened and ruined everything. For a moment she was mad at everyone around her: her sisters and other random people. 'Stupid mission,' she said quietly.

'Mummy, does this letter say that we will have to move out of Auntie's apartment?'

'No, Frank. It is about something different,' she responded quickly.

'Ok. That's good. Because I really like Aunt Helen, and also I can see in your eyes that you are very happy to be with your sisters. I have never seen you like this before.'

***

Mary's phone rang. 'Hello, Mary speaking,' she answered.

'You killed him, you know! You killed him! It is all because of you!' a female voice was shouting over the phone.

'Who is this? Commissioner?' Mary asked.

'If it hadn't been for you, we would have been able to end his suffering much more quickly. Now he died in pain, like an animal. You are so cruel! You killed him!' the voice was still shouting and crying at the same time.

'I'm sorry to hear about your loss,' Mary replied. That was the best thing she could come up with under the circumstances. This was not the best time to argue with the commissioner.

'I don't give a shit if you are sorry or not, you let him suffer. You killed him! You are like your father …Yes, I know who you are. I remember your father talking during a UN General Assembly. I remember how much hate and aggression was in that speech. I'm glad that he is not alive anymore, there is no place for those types of people in this world,' she continued to shout.

'How can you say that? You knew my father?' Mary asked, and was very surprised by what she was hearing.

'Your whole family is the same. You want people to suffer because you think it is good for them,' she shouted, crying.

'No, I don't think this is what my father was saying …' Mary tried to defend him.

'You can defend him, you were probably too small to even understand what he was saying. The most evil man in the world. I hope you suffer before your death like Mark did …' she cried harder and hung up.

'Wow. That was unexpected,' Mary said, looking at her cell phone. For some reason Mary stayed very calm. She couldn't fully understand why the commissioner blamed her for the death of her lover. She had voted for euthanasia, after all. Maybe she had some hope after all,' Mary thought.

After a few minutes the whole situation finally started to get to Mary. She sat there drinking coffee and thinking about the phone call. 'What if she is right? And I'm responsible for the death of this human being, in such pain? Maybe at the end of the day this euthanasia actually helps people to die in peace, with less suffering,' she said to herself, starting to feel bad about it. But she didn't really know what to do. She had messed up her mission anyway. There was really no hope she could change anything anymore now. 'What if Eugene is suffering as well? I made him that way because of my suspicion and now I'm thinking about euthanasia – really, Mary?' she could not believe her own thoughts. Seconds later another thought came into her head. 'What did she say about my father?' she asked herself and started to do research about him on the internet.

'Nothing there, not even a word,' she said to herself. She was not able to find any recordings, or even any notes about her father giving a speech at the UN General Assembly in 2030.

'It is weird, it's like someone just wiped the whole thing from the net ...' she thought. A few seconds later her son came to her and said, 'Mum, Dad wanted to say something and I wrote it down, please have a look, I am not sure what it means,' the little boy said as he gave a piece of paper to Mary. Eugene was sitting in his wheelchair a few metres away.

'Were you following me when I had the accident?' she read on the piece of paper. Mary burst into tears. Eugene saw, and it was the answer he had been expecting. He looked at her, and she looked into his eyes with sadness. She regretted this very much, but she could not turn back time.

'I'm sorry Mummy. I didn't want to write anything bad,' Johnny said as he hugged and kissed his mum.

'It is just fine, Johnny, don't worry.' Mary tried to stop crying. It was a bit of an awkward situation. She didn't really know what to do. 'Is apologising enough? For ruining a person's life ...' she thought. 'I'm a murderer, a few minutes ago I was thinking about euthanasia,' she thought. She was ashamed of having those thoughts. This was pretty far from the perfect family life she had hoped she would have. She quickly called the nanny and asked her to come over earlier that day. She wanted to escape from the house as soon as possible. She decided to go to Helen's place. She knew that all her sisters had had a very interesting day. She felt that it would be easier to cope with all of this if they were all together. And she was so interested in that speech of her father's, but she couldn't search for it from home.

It was already evening when Mary got to Helen's apartment. All three of her sisters were sitting on the couch in complete silence. This was how their broken lives, careers and dreams affected them. Mary had suspected that the situation might look like this and had brought a bottle of red wine. She was thinking about mixing milk and honey as their mum used to make when they were upset, but red wine was known for centuries as the best remediation to all sadness.

'This will cheer you up a bit,' she said to them and poured the wine into the glasses. They had a quick chat about their horrific days and started looking for their father's speech again.

'I found something on the dark web,' Constance suddenly said.

'Let's have a look then, could you put it on the big screen?' Helen asked. They all sat down on the couch with topped-up glasses of wine and started watching. The video wasn't great quality but it seemed to be the only video online. Nicholas Murphy started his speech:

'Dear people of the world. Thank you for giving me the opportunity to speak to all of you today on behalf of many people to whom Christian, Muslim and Jewish values are important. We have already killed and destroyed our natural habitat. We have killed animals that our robots will not be able to replace. We have destroyed forests and water supplies. Soon enough we'll be fighting for air to breathe and water to drink. We cannot do the same to humanity. I don't think that we need a nuclear war to wipe out our population. We are already working on it, wearing white gloves, to slowly kill our values, which are the basis for human existence. I do appreciate how humanity has evolved over the centuries. Great technological achievements have helped us to be more efficient, effective and more perfect human beings.

But that is actually the problem. We are trying to be perfect. Almost like robots. But we are humans, we are weak, we make mistakes, and we are still more than robots. We have souls that make us cry at the most awkward moments. We have feelings, we love other people and have friends. We are not perfect, we are a mystery, we are God's creation.

I know we have a lot of trouble accepting this truth. That we can be dependent on others. But we are, God gave us our first breath and will give us our last. If we are going to give that breath to ourselves then we will be just another innovation that came from human hands. At the same time, we normalise things. We say: 'This is normal now'. We push some ideologies and make them normal, saying that this is just a result of great human progress. We are becoming gods who can decide about everything.

Humanity has turned into a hierarchy of gods, with some having power over others and freedom being understood as people doing whatever they want. We are living in an autocracy where higher-level gods are making decisions about others. We are taking the best things from humanity to make everyone the same as everyone else. To be standardised, like in an efficient process in a factory. We have lost our understanding of what is natural and normal and what is not. What was on earth when God created this world and what the truth is now. We are slowly killing ourselves, our families. We are trying to be politically correct, manipulating people's minds and feelings. We are giving the power of deciding what is true, and not true, what is good and what is evil, to private companies, who use that power to win people over and profit from their lack of awareness.

I'm addressing you all in this speech. We are changing the world. We are forcing governments to change their laws, which will have a huge impact on the societies we will see in the future. It will have an impact on our children and how they perceive the world. They will think only in the categories this world thinks in. If it doesn't kill us externally, from outside, our bodies… it will kill us on the inside, our hearts and souls. Our expectations and happiness will die. Our happiness will be programmed and designed so we can buy it like bars of chocolate. This is our final call, to stop and look back. To stop and save our civilisation. From a technological perspective we are reaching for the stars, but in terms of humanity and civilisation we are growing closer to animals.

We need to be careful because we can easily cross the line, to a place where a minority will discriminate against the majority, and base their existence on the fact that they can prove that they are not discriminating against minorities. If they are, they have no right to exist in this world.

We all should know the truth about ourselves and this world. I don't want my daughters to fight with others over the truth. For others to attack them because of the truth, or even for defending the truth. The truth will remain until the end of the world, no matter what. I want my daughters to find out the truth about themselves, to question the truth of this world, and find faith within themselves.'

'What is the truth?' someone shouted from the crowd, but no one could disturb Nicholas.

'Fifteen years ago on this stage, courageous leaders were trying to save the environment and our natural habitat. They were not successful. Money and power won. History has forgotten their names. I'm not here to make history; I'm here to give you the power of the Word, which can change lives. The truth will set you free! Amen.'

The girls were pretty shocked by this speech. They didn't say anything; they just kept staring at the screen.

'That was an amazing speech,' said Mary.

'Yeah, truth. Very powerful. Let's watch it again, not sure If I got everything what he said.' said Constance. They watched it a few more times. It wasn't long, it was interesting and they really missed their Dad, so it was good to see his face. At one point they even saw Mum sitting somewhere in the audience.

'There is a note under the clip,' said Helen and started reading:

This movie is not available on any video website on the internet. It can't be found with most search engines. Once again I'm uploading this to the dark web. Before it was gone after a few weeks. Mr Murphy died a few weeks after giving that speech, along with his wife. It was an 'accident', and according to the FBI no third parties were involved. Mr Murphy wasn't the greatest personality of the century. He was a simple man, not a great leader. He said many times that he was doing all of this because he loved his wife, his daughters and friends. Obviously we understand love in different ways, and for some of you this is not love at all. But he believed in this, and gave everything he had in his life to ensure that his family and friends were happy. If this is not love, then I don't know what is.

The Murphy sisters felt the power of the words their father had proclaimed. Those words gave them some confidence and hope, which was unexpected in their situation. It was not over, they thought. They wanted to fight until the end.

10

Simone took an overnight flight to Boston. The next morning she meant to go to court to discuss custody arrangements with her husband. The flight was not too long, but she could not sleep. The wind was horrific and the airplane was shaking like a ship on the ocean. It was very uncomfortable and terrifying for some. The cabin pressure changed a few times, and people felt like there was a drop in altitude from time to time. It was not ideal for people with stomach problems. Simone was not a frequent flyer either, but her stomach was not so sensitive. She had also tried not to eat before the flight in case she got sick. She was prepared for many things. Obviously the weather these days was much less predictable. It changed very often, and extreme weather conditions anywhere in the world were not so rare.

'We have passed an area with extreme turbulence. You can relax now and enjoy the rest of this flight to Boston,' the Captain said

'Wow … finally, only a half an hour left … not sure how much longer I could have gone without using the toilet. Excuse me,' said a black-haired man sitting beside Simone.

'Of course,' Simone stood up and let the man pass.

'Miss, would you like anything to drink?' the flight attendant asked Simone.

'No, thank you,' she responded automatically. 'Or, wait. I will have a quick gin and tonic with mint and blueberries.' She was tired. The other reason why she could not sleep was that she was thinking about what would happen in the court in the morning. She knew that it would be an upsetting event. So this gin and tonic might relax her a bit before she got there.

'Here you go,' the flight attendant responded as she brought her the drink very quickly.

'Thank you,' Simone responded and had a quick first sip. 'This is what I needed,' she said to herself, smiling at the glass. Seconds later, the man who was sitting next to her came back from the restroom. She drank quickly. She hoped that the drink would put her to sleep.

They landed with only a ten-minute delay. Considering the weather conditions on the way, it wasn't bad. She was glad to be back in Boston. She had spent a lot of her life there, and she really enjoyed the city. It wasn't like New York was bad or anything, but the atmosphere was different. Everyone was rushing to work, school, everywhere. And Boston was different. Young, because of the many students, and fresh. You could literally smell fresh vegetables and flowers on the streets. Of course this was changing because of the unavailability of plants, flowers and vegetables, but the mayor always tried to take an interest in the environment and tried to maintain some green spaces in Boston.

It was difficult for Simone to wake up. She had slept for only about fifty minutes. It was still early in the morning, just about getting to 5 a.m., but she could not go back to sleep. The case in court would start at 8 a.m., so she wanted to be fresh and ready. She had a quick shower at the airport and a large Americano to wake her up.

She was ready, or at least that was what she thought. She got a cab and went directly to the court. She was not planning to stay overnight in Boston. She didn't really have any place to stay, and staying under the same roof as Marcus was not an option for her. Her flight back to JFK was at 9 p.m. She hoped that she could visit her favourite coffee shop before she returned to New York.

She managed to avoid any traffic jams and was pretty early getting to court. She sat down and finished her coffee. A few minutes before 8 a.m. Marcus showed up. He was not late, but not early either, and as far as she could remember, for other cases he was usually much earlier. Maybe he just didn't want to talk to her for too long.

'Hi,' he said very coldly.

'Hi,' Simone responded with little emotion as well.

'How is Frank?' he asked.

'Now you care! He is great!' She was annoyed already with his games. He had never asked about Frank when they were living in the same house.

'Good,' Marcus responded, keeping his nerves under control.

'Next case!' someone shouted and Simone and Marcus entered the courtroom and took their seats.

'So we have a divorce and custody case,' said the judge

'Divorce?' Simone sounded surprised.

'I believe Mr Kelly is representing himself. What about you, Mrs Kelly?' the judge asked.

'Apologies Your Honour, but I don't think I'm ready for this. I didn't know that it was a divorce hearing and that I would need a lawyer. I thought it would be straightforward,' she responded.

'Ok. Not sure what was in the letter that you obviously received, because you are here, but we need to start proceeding. We can find another time when you are better prepared, but we have to at least listen to the person who initiated this proceeding. Mr Kelly you can start. Please give us your justification.' The judge was very polite and calm.

'Of course, Your Honour. Here are the three reasons why I have submitted the papers filing for divorce and full custody of our child, Frank. First, she cheated on me. She was meeting with other men, and was unfaithful to me.'

'What?!' Simone shouted. 'What are you saying? That is not true!' Simone could not calm down.

'Mrs Kelly, please calm down. We will be discussing all of those in detail, but not now.' The judge was still very calm.

'Thank you, Your Honour,' Marcus continued. 'Secondly, she wanted to destroy my career, and create bad publicity for me and my clients. Thirdly, and this is related to filing for full custody over Frank, she is just a bad mother and I have examples of her behaviour that show that she is far from being an ideal mother.'

'How could you say that, you bastard?' Simone shouted.

'Mrs Kelly, please calm down. Once again, we don't want to call security.'

'Apologies, Your Honour.' Simone calmed down a bit.

'Fair enough. So we have everything now, and we can proceed. We will meet again in two weeks. Mrs Kelly, please be prepared next time. Mr Kelly, please share all your evidence with Mrs Kelly and her lawyers. Case closed for today. Thank you.' The judge left the courtroom. Simone jumped out of her seat and attacked Marcus.

'How could you do that to me? I have never cheated on you. I was faithful. Why are you lying? You will never get Frank! Never!' Simone shouted in his face.

'You will see all my evidence, then we can talk. Let me know when you have a lawyer, so I can send everything over. Unless you can't find a lawyer,' he laughed, and left the courtroom.
Simone calmed down after a minute and tried to be a bit more rational.

'I need to find a lawyer,' she thought. It was a bit difficult as all the lawyers in town knew Marcus really well, and the ones she knew were his best mates, so that was a no-go. Straight after the court visit she went to a few law firms to find a lawyer.
Unfortunately, when they heard Marcus Kelly's name, most refused to represent her. She decided to send a quick message to the group chat with her sisters:
'Morning, Murphy gang! Need your help. Need a lawyer to represent me in court, and I can't get

anyone in Boston because they all know Marcus. Any tips?'

She got some names quickly. She scheduled meetings with them. All were based in New York, so she had some time to herself in Boston. She went to her favourite coffee shop and ordered another Americano. 'What evidence does he have that I have cheated on him?' she wondered. I have never done anything like that, so this has to be a big lie,' she thought. She knew that this wouldn't be as easy as she had thought. It would get ugly. She started thinking about what evidence she might have against Marcus. Because attack is the best defence, as they say. But it was not easy to get any. She was not living in the house anymore. And Marcus knew how to hide everything.

***

Mary's relationship with Eugene changed. He had received the answer to his question and it seemed like it had been very disappointing and upsetting to him. Mary wondered how he actually knew about it; it had been a very random question. She thought that maybe someone had given him the idea.

'Who would do that?' she asked herself. She decided to walk to work that morning. The childminder came earlier than usual, so she decided to leave earlier as well. The weather was fine. It looked like the tough weather conditions had only lasted as long as Simone's flight. Most of the time the weather was pretty decent, not even too cloudy.

There was another reason to take a walk that morning: the speech she had seen last night with her sisters. Her father's speech. She was amazed, because she had not seen Dad again after she had left home. She remembered him a bit differently.

She was also very curious about what he had been saying there on the stage. At the start it made no sense to her, but when they watched it over and over again it started to make some sense. She was very into technology, that was obvious, because of her professional role and interests, but at the same time she was not blind and she saw all of the dangerous things that could happen if humans lost control over AI, data mining and machine learning. Or if those things got so complicated and complex that single human beings couldn't manage them anymore.

When she got to the office she felt great. The healthy walk had produced some endorphins, so in spite of the issues that she had had to deal with recently she felt happy. At least right then.

With the coffee that she got on her way to the office, she sat at her desk, and started reading emails. An invitation popped out of her calendar. An 'urgent chat' with her VP. 'Probably some systems that are down,' she thought.

She started looking at her emails. She had a little backlog because of her current private situation. She hadn't really paid much attention to what was happening at work over the last couple of weeks and months. She was always somewhere else with her thoughts. After thirty minutes of searching, she gave up. 'Nothing there,' she said, looking at her inbox. 'Let's see what he has to say.' She stood up and went to the meeting room.

'Hi Robert' she said when a grey-haired 55-year-old man showed up on the screen.

'Hi Mary, hope you are doing well,' he responded quickly.

'Yes, pretty ok. What's going on? It sounds from the tone of your invite like something is falling apart,' she said and smiled, thinking that this was probably not as urgent as he thought.

'Yeah, it is not related to systems failing or operational issues …' he started.

'Re-org, then?' she asked.

'Not that, either,' he responded.

'Ok Robert, keep going, I'm interested.' She sat down more comfortably.

'Yes. So for the last few weeks or even months we have been getting some feedback from your team members as well as from other people in the company,' he said

'Feedback is good. I guess it is about me. Bring it on. I'm all for continuous improvement,' she replied and smiled.

'I appreciate your good humour, but the feedback was really negative and the decision has been made to terminate your contract immediately,' he said

'What? Are you serious? How negative was that feedback?' she was shocked.

'There are some reports that you were talking about very controversial topics in a way that is not acceptable in our workplace. People felt offended and felt that those views and opinions are not part of our culture. That pretty much sums it up,' he said

'Wait a second. What topics? And by the way, I thought we were very open here to different points of view,' she responded

'No, some, let's call them "religious views" are in total contradiction to what we believe in here. Let's be honest, Christianity, and other religions for that matter too, concern only a minority of people these days. They will die pretty soon, because their views are just not acceptable to modern society.'

'I disagree,' she responded

'Sure, I don't really care. It was great to have you on our team, you were a great professional but you crossed a line,' he said calmly.

'Yeah, well, Robert, that is only your opinion. For a long time when I was working here, I was searching for my real identity as a human being. And I found it. Christian values are the closest to my heart. And I won't be hiding it. So your bad, I guess. The other thing is, I don't recall – and you know that I have a pretty good memory – when I ever talked about these topics. Any clues?'   she asked knowing the answer to this question.

'I don't know. I just got a report from HR, so no idea. Mike will help you to pack your stuff and will collect your things that were provided by the company, like your cell phone and laptop. Bye.' Robert hung up. Mary was left alone in the room. She felt paralyzed.

'Nice. So I have no job now. I'm wondering how they got this data. Someone had to be listening to my conversations with sisters, outside of work. That's pretty bad, but can I prove it?' she thought, sitting in the meeting room and looking at her laptop.

Mary scheduled some time with the HR team. She wanted to know what exactly was in those reports. HR hesitated for a moment, but they knew that under the law they were obligated to do it, so they passed over all the feedback, obviously without names.

Mary read through it and felt that it was more like a secret intelligence report than feedback from peers. Unfortunately she couldn't do much. She could sue them, but that was risky. As Robert had said, Christianity was dead in this world, there was no chance that she would be able to convince the judge to uphold her rights. Another thing was that she didn't really want to work for a company that had values that were so different from hers. It would blow up one day anyway.

She cleaned out her desk and found her laptop and phones. She printed out the report and feedback just to have a copy of her own and read through it again more carefully.

She didn't want to stay in the office for too long. She felt embarrassed by the way people were looking at her. Even when people came to her to say hello, or bye, or good luck … she knew that they all knew why she had been let go. She was not embarrassed of the views she had, but of what holding them had become. Words of power and eternal happiness had become unpopular and not suitable for smart and modern twenty-first century society.

***

'It is unbelievable how everything started falling apart in our lives,' said Helen, standing by the window with a coffee in her hands and looking out the window of her apartment.

'Wow, you're having very philosophical thoughts at 7 a.m. in the morning,' Conny responded, barely opening her eyes.

'Sorry Sis, I thought you were awake. Are you not going for a jog this morning?' Helen asked.

'No, I need a break sometimes. Maybe tomorrow,' Conny responded with a sleepy voice after sitting up in bed.

'The last few weeks and months have been so crazy …' Helen continued.

'Yep, there is a lot going on in this world,' Conny agreed, grabbing a coffee from the kitchen.

'Not even just that, look at our stories. We met again after so long, we got some missions that seemed to be interesting and important. During the course of these missions we found ourselves! Or at least I did. And we talked a lot, and I think we got to know each other much better. It was a great time, but now everything is falling apart. I have no work, Simone has to fight to keep her son, Mary lost her job and is depressed, you are in trouble. And yet in all that we seem to be holding on' Helen said

'Yeah, I know what you mean. I don't really worry too much about my troubles because I've been constantly in trouble since I was 14 years old, so no big change for me …' she paused for a moment. 'But you know what I was thinking? That it would be very difficult for us to deal with those problems on our own. At least now we have each other and we can support each other.' Conny walked over to Helen and hugged her.

'Thank you Conny. This is important, and problems seem much smaller when we have each other.' Helen kissed her cheek.

'Oh, I almost forgot. When I was in our old house some time ago, I found this box with Mum's things. I was in a rush so I haven't really looked into it yet. Let's check it out now,' Conny said and went to check her bag. She had a bit of rubbish in her bag, as usual, but after a minute she found what she was looking for.

'Here it is.' Conny smiled and took it out of the bag.

It was a wooden box covered in yellow tape, and it looked like it had probably been made by their mum. It had some very interesting stickers on it and some letters. It wasn't opened. Conny looked at the box. 'I haven't even opened it. I don't know how to open it, really,' she said, and showed it to Helen.

'Maybe you need something to open it with? Eye scan? Finger scan? A password?' Helen asked.

'Not sure, I can't see anything here. There is just a hole here, this has to be very old,' Conny responded.

'A hole? Maybe we need a key …' Helen paused for the moment. 'I might have an idea where we can find this key,' she said after a second, got up and went to open a drawer.

'Before Mum was arrested, she gave me a key. She said that she expected someone to look for it one day and I should hide it.' She took out the key, and put it into the keyhole in the box. It worked. The box was a similar colour inside. There was a notepad inside, some souvenirs, and also some old photographs.

'I think this is us, when we were kids.' Helen looked at the photos and tears ran down her face. 'Those photographs are really touching,' she said, looking at a Christmas picture taken when they had all been sitting at the dinner table.

'Yeah, so lovely. Good times,' added Conny. 'Let's see what is written on the notepad,' she said and opened it.

'Looks like Mum's diary or something,' Helen said.

'Yep, there is a title even, on the second page. "Diary of a Broken Soul",' Conny read. 'I wonder if she suffered because of some disease or if it was just the world that broke her heart and soul?' Helen thought out loud.

'I would suggest looking inside,' responded Conny. 'I would not normally read other people's diaries, but it seems like we were meant to read it, and we were meant to find it because we had the key, so maybe Mum wanted us to read it. Let's do it.' Conny opened another page and   started reading:

'Trust in God's mercy,' we always thought, or maybe the Old Testament made us believe this – that God punished people who sinned and rewarded the good ones. But when we read the story of Job, we must wonder, how is it possible that God punished him if he didn't do anything wrong? He was an extraordinary man.

We quickly forget that it doesn't matter how bad our sins were, God's mercy is still bigger than the cruellest sin. We should remember, as well, that God is not punishing anyone. Original sin, our nature and the consequences of our sins punish us.

We should always trust that God loves us and that He wants the best for us. We should not think otherwise when bad and scary things happen to us, He still wants what is good for us, and our happiness. He wants us to accept his salvation and real freedom. Sometimes we are blind to all of His works in our lives. Every meeting with a person is His gift, and He is trying to give us His love through other people. When you realise truly that this is the truth in your life you won't listen to evil, and you will find safety and happiness. God gave us His own Son to suffer and die for us. Imagine that!

'Wow. That was pretty strong,' Helen said. 'Let me read something now,' she said as she took the diary from Conny. 'She titled each page, so let's find an interesting topic.' She skipped a few pages and opened the diary again on a light blue page.

'"Loneliness",' she read.

Building relationships with people is important but loneliness can bring happiness as well. We can see that inside of ourselves. We see that there is a part of our hearts that we are unable to reveal to other people. Sometimes we cannot even reveal it to ourselves. It seems to be so deep in our hearts and souls.

The world is telling us to escape from loneliness. To not spend time in silence. It is telling us that we should be afraid of loneliness. But at the same time we feel somehow that no one can fulfil everything in our hearts. Silence helps us to understand our deepest awareness of our existence. Only then we can make good, and well-thought out decisions. But we prefer to escape from this loneliness. It is a consequence of Original Sin. We understand loneliness as punishment and that is why we are scared of it. If we don't accept this part of life, we won't be able to truly love others. We will only use other people to give us a taste of happiness. Only in the silence of your loneliness will you meet your true self and God.

Helen finished reading.

'Those texts are pretty impressive, to be honest, but I would have to read them again to see if I agree' said Conny. 'I don't remember Mum reading them to us, maybe I was just too young to talk about those things,' she added.

Someone knocked at the door.

'I wonder who is here so early in the morning.' Helen asked and got up from the couch.

'Maybe a neighbour,' Conny said.

Helen opened the door and found Jane's father standing there looking pretty unhappy, angry even. He didn't say a word, he just entered the apartment.

'Hey, what are you doing? Helen was not happy about him coming in without being invited in. She was actually pretty annoyed with his behaviour, considering that he had bumped into her when coming inside.

'I fucking told you once and I won't repeat myself again. Stay away from my daughter! Don't give her advice, don't talk to her!' he shouted at them.

'Please calm down, there is a child sleeping here.' Conny was thinking about Frank, who had been left with his aunties for the day while Simone was in Boston.

'Stop telling me what to do! I don't appreciate you talking to my daughter when I told you to stop doing that, to your face, a week ago!' he shouted again at Helen.

'What are you talking about? I didn't talk to her. You are mistaken,' Helen answered.

'Maybe not you, maybe your troublemaker sister!' he shouted, even louder and angrier.

'She is not a troublemaker. She can't talk to her anyway, she doesn't have her cell number. Right, Conny?' Helen asked

'Yeah, I don't have her cell number …' Conny paused

'You see!' Helen shouted.

'But I was talking to her,' Conny responded

'What? How come? Where?' Helen asked

'The other day when you were in the shower, someone rang. I saw her name come up on the phone, and decided to answer … she was crying. I said to wait for you but she sounded very upset, and I thought she might do something so I decided to talk to her in the meantime.' Conny felt a bit embarrassed.

'Why didn't you tell me?' Helen asked

'Because I left the apartment right after you came out of the bathroom and just forgot,' Conny responded.

'And did you tell your sister about the abortion you had?' the man asked.

'How do you know that?' Conny was surprised

'Abortion? When?' Helen was worried.

'My daughter is depressed now, because both of you stupid women talked to her and confused her even more. You were no help to her at all. And you!' he pointed at Conny 'I will sue you for all of this, for ruining her life!' he shouted again. Seconds later he turned around, walked back out through the open front door and left the apartment. He was gone.

'Yikes, I'm in deep shit now,' Conny said. 'I'm sorry Helen, it didn't work out the way I wanted. I'm pretty bad at making friends and building good relationships.' Helen understood. She came close to Conny, looked into her eyes and hugged her.

'Don't worry, Sis. You are not alone anymore with all of this. Your problems are my problems as well. We will sort them out together.' Helen smiled. 'But I think we have a bit more catching up to do,' she added, looking at Conny with questioning eyes, wanting to know about the abortion she had had.

***

When Mary left the office, someone from the company escorted her. That was the usual procedure. She left behind all company belongings like laptops and phones and packed her own things. She left her badge at reception. Simon, her coworker who was escorting her to the door, only said: 'I'm sorry it has ended like this. I hope you will be successful in the future.' He tried to smile.

'Yeah, that sounds very fake. Is this the message HR told you to give me in their email when they asked to escort me to the door?' she asked.

'Yeah, kind of …' he said, and looked ashamed.

'Haha,' she laughed 'That is actually very funny,' she added. 'Tell me, what is this all about? Is it really about views that don't suit the company?' she asked

'No. I don't think so. There was a survey a while ago about you, and I think the main impression here was that in recent weeks you had lost your focus on things that are important for the company and you kind of lost your ability to be a good leader.' Simon was very honest.

'How come?' Mary asked

'You are just too soft these days … and they needed someone more ruthless, I guess,' he added.

'I'm glad it is not about Christianity, I would be very mad if it was that,' she said.

'No, I don't think anyone cares about Christianity or any other religion these days. We are the gods nowadays, we create, we decide who lives and who dies, we own the future of humanity,' he laughed. 'Good luck!' he threw those honest words in at the end and left.

'Wow. I heard that before, it gave me a fright, because of the way you said it.' Mary quickly got into Waymo's car and drove home.

This was not an easy day. They were all waiting for Simone to come back. Frank was missing her big time, which was not strange but it had only been one day. He refused to go to sleep until Mummy was back. So they sat on the couch, aunties opened a nice bottle of wine, and enjoyed this time together.

'I probably should be crying, because I lost my job, but I won't, I guess it was time for a change,' Mary said to her sisters

'You will be alright, Sis, you are the smartest of all of us,' Helen said.

'I agree,' added Conny and raised her glass to Mary's. 'Cheers!' she shouted.

Simone came home at around 9 p.m. She was tired, because again she hadn't really slept on the plane.

'Are we celebrating something?' she asked with a smile when she got in and saw her sisters drinking wine.

'We always are, Sis. We celebrate ourselves! This is what we have, and who we are!' Helen responded.

Frank ran to Simone and jumped into her arms. 'I missed you, Mummy. You were away for so long!' he said.

'I missed you too, Frankie.' Simone kissed her little boy. 'What a crazy day it's been.' Simone looked at her sisters and then at her cell phone. 'Oh, here you go,' she exclaimed.' She sounded excited.

'What's happened?' Conny asked.

'Marcus emailed me the evidence, I need to pass it on to my lawyer,' she responded.

'What's in there?' Mary asked.

Simone didn't have to explain much. She had already chatted with each of them during the day. She sat down beside them. Conny gave her a glass of wine as well.

'I guess you might need this,' she said to her. Simone had a sip and started looking into the files Marcus had sent over. 'Oh my … what a jerk!' She was looking at some pictures of herself when she had been at the park with Frank. 'I can't believe this. These are pretty old photographs, which caught me in weird situations with Frankie,' she said.

'Can I see?' Frank asked.

'No, little boy, I think it is time for you to go to sleep now. I love you so much.' Simone left the phone on the couch for a moment and gave Frank a kiss on his forehead. 'Goodnight my love,' she said and smiled. When Frankie left she went back to the couch and her sisters. She looked at more files.

'I have no idea why he has these pictures, these were taken a long time before we wanted to break up. It seems like he was already preparing for this divorce,' Simone commented.

'What a di- I mean, donkey,' Conny stopped herself as she was not sure if Frankie was already asleep or not.

'What the hell is that?!' Simone shouted. There were some photographs of her kissing someone. 'It cannot be me. I don't know this man. I have never been in this place.' Simone was disappointed.

'We believe you, Simone,' her sisters responded together.

'Thank you, that means the world to me,' she replied with a smile. 'But how can I convince the judge that it wasn't me? I really need a good lawyer.

11

And she got one, at least she hoped that he was a good one. His name was Sean Kavanagh. He was from Boston originally and had studied with Marcus at Harvard Law School, but they hadn't liked each other too much. And this was Simone's last chance. Not only did he want to beat Marcus Kelly, but he was actually a pretty good lawyer, and the only one who didn't refuse to take the case. Marcus was pretty well known in the Boston area. Many lawyers were his friends or at least wanted to be on good terms with him. So no one really wanted to go against him. The other thing was that Marcus was actually really good at what he did. His firm was very well known and they had very powerful and big customers.

Unfortunately, Simone found her lawyer pretty late in the process; over a week later and just a week before her case was meant to come up in court again. Still, he was very keen to take it and try at least to win it; he thought there was a chance he could do it.

In the meantime, Simone's sisters decided to help her and figure out a strategy for this case. Obviously they had a lot of time on their hands, so they could spend it any way they wanted. For example, they found that detective agency that had taken that picture of Simone kissing another man, and other interesting photographs. It seemed like this agency had a very high rate of getting what customers were looking for. And it seemed like their clients were not particularly interested in knowing the truth, but just wanted confirmation that their suspicions were true. And there's a huge difference between the truth and suspicions. Marcus wanted confirmation that his wife had cheated on him so he could use it against Simone. And they came up with what he paid them for. It seemed very odd that there was a picture of Simone kissing a man she had never seen in her life.

Mary, their expert on technology-related matters, and Conny, the dark web explorer, did some digging and found that those detectives had a very interesting partner company called Faceswap, the main focus of which was on improving graphic technology and recreating the faces of actors, for example. They could literally use the face of an old actor, who was already dead, and have him appear in a new movie. They were really good at doing that, and people could not spot the difference.

Conny found out on the dark web that they had extended their services by building deep fake videos on request. They didn't care who paid, or how, or why they did what they did. They were just doing their job. No hard feelings. They probably had probably done the same thing to Simone, but someone had to prove it, and this was an issue. Using comments from dark web forums is pretty lame evidence. They needed emails, conversations between Marcus and the company. But that seemed almost impossible to find.

'Let's leave it to the lawyer, maybe he will be able to figure out the best way to find that connection,' said Mary.

'Yes. You ok with that Simone?' Conny asked.

'Yeah, fine. I just can't believe that people can do such things and accept money for it. It's immoral.' Simone was really upset.

'Yeah, this world is very upsetting. No one really cares about the truth these days. Money and power are people's goals in life. This generation is actually poorer for it.' Helen added.

'Mummy, where is my toy dinosaur?' Frank suddenly asked Simone.

'Not sure, Frankie. Maybe it is in the box with the other toys. Did you bring it from Boston?' Simone asked Frank.

'Let me see.' Frank went down to his room to check the toy box. 'Nothing here, Mum,' he shouted from his room.

'I will check in Boston when I am there next week.' She tried to cheer Frankie up.

'But I really wanted to show it to Auntie Helen,' he said.

'I think I have some photos and videos from your birthday, you were definitely playing with it then,' Simone said and started looking at her cell phone.

'Here you go, I found it,' she told him as she handed the phone to Frankie, who immediately showed it to Helen. They started watching videos.

'You will see it in a minute,' he said, pointing at the phone screen.

'Here it is!' he shouted when his dinosaur toy showed up. 'I actually have some more videos on my device, I remember now …' he ran off to his room to grab his tablet. He came back after a few seconds, already scrolling and going through hundreds of videos and photographs. 'Look at this video, Auntie. I need to go pee.' He gave her the device and ran off to the bathroom. Helen started watching the video. But there was something strange in the background, a voice, a male voice.

'Can you hear that?' Helen asked her sisters and played the video again.

'It is probably Marcus, I guess Frank made this video when I was here for the first time.' Simone responded.

'But do you hear what he is saying?' Helen asked and played the video one more time.

'We might have evidence against him,' Mary said and smiled.

'What a jerk, talking like this about a mother in front of her child,' Conny added.

'Yeah, well. This is nothing new for him,' Simone responded, and she was not laughing. She had heard similar words many times before from Marcus, but she had never responded to them until recently.

When Simone met Sean Kavanagh two days later, she gave him all the evidence she had, including this video from Frankie's device. He was pretty keen to use it in court, but less happy about the deep fake video. He believed her, and he understood all the comments from the dark web forums, but he could not really use them, and he was not able to find a way to connect Marcus to the two companies. He told Simone that in a previous case he had dealt with these companies and that they had a lot of power, and enough money to not lose cases like this.

A week after her first meeting with her lawyer, Simone went to Boston again. She found the famous dinosaur toy in her old house when she went there while Marcus was out, and then she went to the courtroom with Sean.

'Seriously? Sean Kavanagh? My biggest enemy?' Marcus attacked Simone straight away, showing clearly how unhappy he was with her choice of lawyer.

'Do you seriously think I care?' Simone was calm this time and didn't want to get into a fight.

Unfortunately the case didn't go well for Simone from the start. As far as the judge knew, Simone was cheating on her husband. The court didn't know what deep fake videos were and because they had no evidence that this was what had happened, the only truth was that she had kissed some man on the street.

So the divorce was inevitable but there was still the matter of who would get custody of Frank, and there seemed to be a chance that Simone could win it. Sean used the video evidence from Frank's device well, which really surprised Marcus. With all of

Marcus's evidence showing how bad a mother Simone was, it looked like they were both pretty terrible parents. Suddenly Marcus played his ace … an article from that day's *New York Times*.

'Your Honour I would like to use this article from today's *New York Times* as evidence. He brought the newspaper to the judge.

'We'll take a ten-minute break so we can all read the article, I guess Mrs Kelly has not seen it yet, either,' the judge said and left the courtroom.

'What article?' Sean whispered to Simone.

'I don't know,' she responded.

'I guess you don't have it, so here you go,' Marcus said as he brought two copies to their table and gave them to Sean and Simone, smiling cheekily.

And this was the end. The judge recognised the importance of this article, from such a respected newspaper. He called both lawyers and asked them if they wanted to make a deal. Sean knew that this was the only chance for Simone to see her child at all. So he didn't negotiate, he just took what Marcus gave him. Simone burst into tears when she heard the final verdict. She had lost her child.

***

And what was the article about? It was important, because it changed the Murphy sisters' story again, this time in an even more dramatic way. The article was very well done, professionally written, and easy to read. You could probably question some of the facts that were mentioned, but considering the nature of those kinds of articles and the state the world was in, it was not surprising that some things had been interpreted in some very specific ways. In a nutshell, the whole masterpiece was divided into three parts.

The first went back to 'ancient times' and described Barb and Nicholas Murphy. The descriptions were probably not far from true. They were who they were, and lived the lives they desired to live. The facts were true, but the way they were interpreted and the motivations assumed to be behind their actions were invented. They echoed the way they had been understood in 2030, just before they were killed. Obviously it was not like they were the only great minds out there and the whole world was wrong about them. Surely not. There were many more men and women who thought like they did, but who had never had the courage to say so openly. The article showed them as a madman and a madwoman, and maybe that was accurate, because you needed to be a bit crazy to go against the whole world, just to follow your understanding of truth.

Then the author – Pulitzer prize winner Hans von Schaufarer – slowly started to introduce Barb and Nicholas's children, their four daughters. He began with their childhood, and he already strayed pretty far from reality there. It seemed like he had a format for this article that he was trying to follow, and he twisted some facts just to make his point. One of these was the way Nicholas had taught his children his values and what is important in life. The journalist claimed that they had had no TV or internet when they were kids, and that they were punished if they didn't pray or read the Bible.

The truth was that this would have gone against Barb and Nick's values, if this had been the way they treated religion and faith. Their understanding of living in faith and living a religious life was much deeper than this. By doing things the way it had been described by von Schaufarer they could have killed even the smallest grain of faith in their children's hearts. Finding out the truth about yourself, God and the world around you was the most important thing for Barb and Nick. Obviously that was taking a risk; that the truth that their girls would find would be different from their own, but they had accepted that risk. They knew that it would be good only if it came from their children's hearts, and that they would eventually find the same truth that Nick and Barb had found years back.

Then the journalist went into the Murphy sisters' current lives. He introduced every one of them, describing briefly what they were doing, how their careers looked and what their families looked like. Even though the Murphy sisters had never been very vocal on social media, probably because they just hadn't wanted to be in the limelight after what had happened with their parents, the article contained many details about their lives, which meant that someone had done a really good job of digging into their lives.

Of course the whole point of this article was not to make them look good, and even they themselves wouldn't have expected an entirely positive description, but listing the sins of each family member was very childish. Like small children arguing in kindergarten. Mary did this, Helen did that. Those were the facts. Mary had been involved in her husband's accident, and she regretted it. Conny and Helen had each had an abortion, for different reasons, but they did. Simone had pretended to be a freelance journalist. But adding interpretations to those facts, which were very inaccurate, showed the girls in a very bad light. They seemed like evil creatures, you would think they were monsters after reading this article. But as everyone knows, the reality is that human beings' characters are not black and white. We have our good sides and bad sides, either one of which sometimes wins the battle of our hearts.

Unfortunately, the last piece of that remarkable story was about the family's impact on the world, and in general about how their Christianity and Christian values were affecting the world. It was very interesting to note that the journalist called those values 'Christian'. Most of what he discussed were really philosophical questions people had asked themselves for centuries and which they had responded to by concluding that it was important to be good and love people.

It seemed like this idea was not standard anymore. And the author was looking at it as if at some ancient, forgotten Christian idea. He very carefully described different issues that he had with those kinds of values. He questioned them very well, and he admitted that he couldn't find his own answer to some of them. At the same time, he explicitly said that the reason he couldn't find an answer was very simple. Christianity didn't matter anymore. He quoted the Bible, and also some Catholic Church documents, but he treated them like ancient texts from which you could learn how people in olden times thought about what life was about and how they had tried to live.

It was like someone from the past coming into our lives and trying to still live their life by values from their own times. It was unacceptable, and governments should do something about it so people's lives were not disturbed. That was his conclusion.

The interesting thing was what he wrote about the impact that the Murphy sisters had had on the world. You would think that with nine billion people in this world, four women who were not established very well in society and did not have big, impactful jobs or roles in this world, would not have much of an impact. Still, the author saw them as a threat to the world. But why? Because they were free, and they were together. He called it 'mad Christian freedom'. Freedom where people followed not their best interest, but followed the mysterious way of their hearts. Those people were capable of doing many unpredictable things. And that was scary to him and he felt that it should be for everyone. This was how the terrorists years back had treated the world. They had attacked people because of their beliefs, they had felt free, and no one could control them. And that was very risky.

Additionally, them being together and supporting each other was not good either. It is easier for the system to fight one person who has their own goals and dreams. Because you can change that person, by destroying their dreams or at least controlling them that way. The Murphy sisters had each other, and they supported each other when they failed. As the author wrote in the article, years back you could have said that they were normal and good people. And they hadn't changed much, but today they were far from normal and were actually dangerous because being 'good' had a different meaning now.

This article was a game changer. Not only for Simone's case, but for all of them. Something broke. They knew. It was not a case of simply suffering a little, not a case of temporary issues that they would solve and then there would be a happy ending.

They felt inside their hearts that this time there would be no happy ending. This could only lead in one direction, to the end of their lives. They realised that, and of course it was upsetting and terrifying, because they were still very young. But at the same time, they felt in a mysterious way in their hearts that this place was not their home yet. The journey would continue, no matter what. The article changed their day-to-day lives as well. Every single person in the world felt obligated to post their opinion about those evil, dangerous creatures.

Obviously everything started with the comments below the online version of this article. The servers were so busy that the *New York Times* had to upgrade their servers to allow for more traffic. At the same time, the discussion in the commentary section became so tense that eventually the newspaper blocked the option to comment under the article. But that didn't mean that the commentary stopped. Not at all.

It became a hot topic in the media and the virtual world. It flooded different online channels, TV news, global newspapers, magazines, blogs, etc. Everything. Everyone in the world felt like they had to have their opinion on this subject. More details were uncovered and the lives of the Murphy sisters were scanned by the social media X-ray machine. Some of the facts uncovered were true, some were not, but it didn't matter. It was time to kick them in the stomach, till they were lying on the ground. If you read those comments you might wonder what they had actually done to deserve this kind of treatment in the media.

At one point it got very personal. The articles stopped being only about their views or personal history, and started to be about them as people. Marcus, Greg, the headmaster from Simone's school, the commissioner from the UN, the pro-life campaign leader, they all had their five minutes of fame in the media to tell the truth about who each of the Murphy sisters was. Obviously their opinions were biased but that didn't matter to anyone. They started to be seen as the biggest enemies of humankind. They were personally attacked and embarrassed by comments about their looks, health and characters. This grew into a big story within just a week of the first article being published. The strangest thing was the amount of detail from their private lives that was revealed and used against them. This was not only data known to people because they interacted with them. It was also very personal and intimate information about their browsing history as well as photos, emails and calendar entries. It was the kind of stuff that should not interest anyone.

And where were the defenders of personal data? Human rights?

Nope. Showing up publicly to defend those four women would have been a kind of professional suicide. It was really upsetting to the sisters when they had to hear and read all of these things. They were sitting in the apartment and they had to listen to the crowds that were standing outside and waiting for them.

It really hurt Helen. She felt responsible for the whole mess. She had been so enthusiastic about the whole idea of missions, meeting her sisters and uniting the family and doing something good for this world.

'What have I done to you?' Helen was asking herself, sobbing.

'It is not your fault, Helen,' Simone said, trying to calm her down.

Mary was sitting in the corner in silence. She looked like all her feelings were bottled up inside her, she didn't express them anymore. She was so tired of this situation. The home situation was slowly killing her. She really loved Eugene and John. And she could not see them, because she would get attacked by journalists and freedom defenders if she left the apartment. She was so depressed that responding to anyone about this was just tiring and pointless, so that she preferred to say nothing.

'Maybe someone tricked us with those missions?' Conny asked. She was the only one who was calm about the whole situation. She knew that she was probably not the smartest, not yet, or at least she didn't have life experience like her three sisters. At the same time, she was the only one who was able to use her strength in this situation. She was thinking rationally about the whole thing.

'That's a possibility,' Mary suddenly responded.

'But who would do such a thing? And how would they know that we would fail?' Simone asked.

'Maybe those missions were never meant to be successful,' Conny responded

'How come? Why were we supposed to do them then?' Simone followed up.

'Maybe because those missions changed us?' Helen added, still crying.

'What do you mean?' Simone asked

'I agree,' Conny jumped in. 'Maybe those missions were not designed to actually do anything. They were more for us, so we could improve ourselves, our behaviour, challenge our status quo. We have to admit that the last couple of months really changed who we were. We look at the world differently now. Do you think without those failed missions this would be possible? Sometimes you need to fail so you know how much it hurts and you will feel motivated to not repeat the same thing.'

Someone knocked on the door.

'Police! Open up!' the police officers shouted.

'Now we are in trouble,' Conny shouted.

Helen opened the door and a bunch of police officers entered the apartment.

'You are all under arrest!' They shouted.

'But why?' Conny asked.

'For breaking the law,' the officer responded.

'Wow, you are a smartass, man,' Conny quickly responded, smiling.

'Mind your words, lady!' the officer responded.

'Sure, sure … relax.' Conny was not afraid to speak, even in that situation.

'But really, could you be a bit more specific about why you are arresting us?' Mary asked again.

'Yes. There is an investigation against you all that relates to violating human rights, violating other people's freedom, and treason,' another police officer responded.

'Well, doesn't sound too familiar, but what can you expect,' Mary responded very calmly.

'Treason? For what? National secrets? That is a freaking joke!' Conny was losing her mind.

'Lady, you really need to calm down. If you don't, we will have to calm you down.'

'Okay, okay. I'm good now.' Conny calmed down.

The officers put handcuffs on each sister. In a way Simone was happy that Frankie didn't have to see this in person, at least, because she was almost sure that Marcus would show him the online highlights. When they were going down the stairs, all of their neighbours opened their doors and looked at them. Some said nothing, some shouted something offensive, some more aggressive characters even threw things at them. Similarly, outside the building, before they got into the police cars, people watched them, and shouted. No one had the courage to defend them. They were on their own.

They had to be put into the police van. There were a lot of FBI officers as well, and even a SWAT team, which seemed a bit over the top for four young women. They were treated like terrorists. They were then brought to some kind of secret facility that probably belonged to the CIA, and there they were questioned. The Murphy sisters didn't really know where they were. It looked like some old factory, with red brick walls and broken windows. It didn't seem like a very fancy or busy area, more likely a suburb of New York City. They were scared. It was the first time ever, even for Conny, who had a history with FBI agents, that they found themselves in such an uncomfortable situation.

The agents started questioning them, but separately. A tall, black-haired man in a suit and an even taller woman in a black dress were leading the questioning. Helen was called to be questioned first. The rest of the girls stayed in the other room, and were guarded by the SWAT team. There was really nothing in that room besides a table, a few chairs and a couch. The girls were not allowed to go to the restroom or drink or eat anything before being questioned. Apparently that was an old technique to get witnesses to talk.

'What about our lawyers?' Mary asked the guards.

'It is not our job to answer this question,' a big guy with a gun responded.

Mary didn't really feel confident enough to question the qualifications and responsibilities of those guards, so she left it at that. Unfortunately, Helen didn't hear her saying this, and when she was in the room with the two agents she didn't even ask for a lawyer. And of course the agents did not remind her that she might want one.

The questioning started with the usual stuff. Helen gave them her life history and then they started asking her about her relationship with her sisters and parents. Helen had always been a very open and honest person and she didn't plan to change her approach then, either. So she said what she thought about her parents and told them about her relationship with her sisters. Helen was surprised by the amount of detail they already knew about her and her sisters. Compared to the newspapers, they had deeper knowledge but it was actually also correct, and not like the newspapers' babble.

Helen was pretty relaxed during questioning. She didn't worry too much. She was at that stage where she knew exactly where all of it was leading. And she accepted the fact that this was her destination. She was probably more worried about her sisters. They had their lives, and families in Simone and Mary's case, and a bright future ahead of them. After that incident at school, Helen was depressed and she could not figure out what else she could do with her life besides teaching.

She was finished after forty-five minutes. The SWAT team brought her to another room, but not the same one where the other girls were sitting. This one looked a bit more civilised. There were some snacks, some water and a bathroom. It seemed like each sister was then questioned about the same things – that seemed to be the agents' strategy. They were able to find out which sister was the weakest link as well as confirm some information that they already had and make sure none of the sisters were lying.

Only Mary's questioning was different. She actually demanded to meet with a lawyer. They tried to fool her, but she didn't let them. They said that her sisters had already said everything, so it didn't matter. But Mary was stubborn, she had watched too many crime series on TV when she was a teenager to not know how important these kinds of interviews were.

And of course, her sisters had said everything, but they hadn't lied about anything. They had just given the authorities an advantage in preparing for the court case. After the whole thing ended, the Murphy sisters thought that they would be able to go home. Unfortunately it wasn't so simple. In a very strange way the prison had actually become the safest place for them. The hatred against them had become monumental. People were threatening them online, they wanted to 'beat shit out of them', or stab them to death. It had spun completely out of control.

Because of a decision the court made, they spent another five days in prison before the case was heard in court. Everything was rushed because they had been named the biggest threat in the world to the US and the free world. Mary wanted to ask the lawyer she knew personally to represent them. He even agreed, but then resigned for no reason. Most likely he was scared, or when he saw the evidence he knew that this wasn't a battle he could win. Finally they sent a rookie lawyer from the justice department to represent them.

'Hi, my name is Peter Chan. I will be your lawyer,' said the man as he stood in the door of the sisters' cell.

'How old are you?' Mary asked, looking at his young face.

'Twenty-five,' he responded.

'Have you actually graduated from law school?' Conny added.

'Are you questioning my competence?' Peter was a bit annoyed with that question.

'No, just wondering,' Conny responded calmly.

'Yes, I graduated from Columbia Law School two months ago,' he responded.

'Congrats!' Simone exclaimed.

'And how many cases have you won in your career?' Mary asked.

'I haven't won any, to be honest,' he responded quickly. 'Because this is my first case,' he added.

'That's great. We appreciate your honesty. At least you haven't lost any cases yet, so we are on track,' Mary tried to joke a bit because it seemed like a ridiculous situation.

'And you are not planning to run away, right?' Conny asked

'I have seen some documentation, evidence, and I heard your story on the news …' he paused for a second. 'I will be honest with you …we probably won't win it, it seems like in this case you're not only going up against the prosecutor, but the whole world. There is a lot of pressure around this case. But, well, I have hope,' he said, smiling.

'I'm glad you do. What hope is that? Share it with us?' Simone asked.

'I do hope I can get the death penalty off the table,' he said, sounding very confident.

Helen burst into tears when she heard that. And it was not for herself, but for her sisters' lives.   She felt responsible for getting her sisters into this situation.

'You don't have to share so many details with us in the future, that was a bit upsetting, as you can see.' Mary pointed at Helen.

'Of course. I will try my best to do whatever I can to get you out of this mess.'

'Thank you! That's the spirit, let's start and get to work!' Mary, as the eldest, felt a bit responsible for the whole thing.

Peter spent long hours with the Murphy sisters in their prison cell. They went through all the evidence, witnesses, comments, documentation. They prepared for the worst. It was time to confront the whole world, and to find the truth.

12

As expected, the trial was watched by many people around the world. To accommodate the interest of the public, the decision was made that the trial would take place at the New York State Supreme Court. Many TV stations and online media lined up very early on a Monday morning to have the best place from which to start their live stream.

Random people started gathering outside the building early so they could be close enough to shout their opinions about those four villains. No one really expected such a big gathering, so some of the surrounding streets had to be shut down to allow people to stand outside and freely give their opinion.

US courts were usually not keen to show live streams from courtrooms, but this time they had made an exception. The demand and interest were so high that the leading judge was afraid that the crowd outside, as well as people watching videos on social media, might become impatient and actually storm the building.

This was why he allowed the two main US TV stations and three online media providers to live stream directly from the courtroom. Obviously the whole idea had been sold to the public in great packaging. Huge video screens had been installed in many countries, in the main squares of many cities. Everyone wanted to see this trial, everyone wanted to be a part of this moment in history where real truth was expected to win, where the freedom of human beings was expected to win over damaging ideology.

Of course this was a great deal for certain companies, and they were already counting their profits in billions of dollars. This was meant to be the biggest event of the century. To the Murphy sisters it didn't feel like that. They had spent the last couple of weeks in prison, so they had been far from these disturbing voices, politics and marketing.

When they entered the courtroom, they looked very calm. Nobody could see hope in their eyes. No, they didn't hope for anything. They didn't look excited about the public and publicity either. Some celebrities would say: it doesn't matter what they say about you, what matters is that they talk about you at all. But no, it had never been their plan to be on the first page of the newspapers, in the online magazines, on TV shows. They were just simple human beings trying to live their lives according to their beliefs. Figuring out their beliefs had taken them so long that it was so wrong to think that they had been like that from the beginning because they had it in their genes.

'I would like to ask for the first statement on both sides,' the leading judge asked.

'Your Honour,' started the prosecutor, Kennedy. 'We are here because these four sisters wanted to destroy freedom and peace in this world. Inspired by ideologies and religious beliefs they wanted to impact global societies. They wanted to force their understanding of real love and truth on people's ways of thinking, and take from them their freedom, for which we fought for so many years. Their actions are an example of a very specific form of terrorism. They were building a society of fear, and the consequences of those actions might lead people to develop mental illnesses and could lead to their deaths, which has been proven scientifically. Your Honour, we don't see any chance of them changing their behaviour, as we will prove by showing scientific evidence related to their genes. This is why we ask for the death penalty by injection,' he finished and sat down.

As much as they understood the threat of the death penalty and had heard about it so many times already, this time it was different, more terrifying. This was real. You could see the fear in their eyes. The fear of losing their lives but also the fear of leaving behind those who they cared the most about.

'Thank you, Mr Kennedy. Mr Chan, please?' the judge asked Peter for his statement.

'Your Honour, this whole thing sounds like a reality show. Is this the world for which the great leaders of our world fought? Have we completely lost our minds and stopped understanding what words like truth, freedom and love mean? The constitution guarantees every citizen free speech. My clients are pleading not guilty, they were just doing what their hearts told them to do.' Peter sat down and smiled at all of the sisters.

'Well, that was a very creative statement, Mr Chan. Let's start then, the public wants to know what freedom, truth and love mean today.'

Both sides tried to use different tactics during the trial: attacking, defending, scientific facts, stats, data coming from the sisters' private lives, just to prove points. The prosecutor called as a witness professor Wiley, a known clinical geneticist. For five hours he tried to convince the judge and jury that these women's genes were similar to their parents'. They were weak and damaged and that was why they should not really be in this world, because they were letting some non-standard uniqueness into this world that could impact other people's genes. Basically their lives themselves were dangerous to society.

Peter tried to present them in a better light. He asked them about positive situations in their lives, what they had achieved, what they had been doing before they got the letters. That was another thing, the mysterious letters. They had disappeared. There was also no recording in the house. The house was actually empty. That was very disturbing for the sisters, as it made them think that this had just been one big set-up. The letters could have saved them, but at this stage, they didn't want that either.

They could lie, or defend themselves by saying that it had just been a mistake. That their thoughts and beliefs might change. Or that they had received instructions from someone to do those things. No. They had never wanted to go this route. Even more, they still wanted to defend the truth they believed in. Peter hoped and advised them that probably the easiest way to get them out of this situation would be to say what the world wanted to hear. But, no, they wanted to tell the truth.

And they did.

When the prosecutor asked Mary what she thought the truth was, she responded:

We all have our truth. Based on our experience, on our character and history. So many things have been building that definition in our hearts. Our families, friends, schools, other people, ourselves, alone with our weaknesses and thoughts. But when you start looking at those factors, you realise that the truth must be something more, something universal for every human being in history. The truth about who we are, the truth about what we are doing here and where we are going. Believe me, we will die, no matter how much we do to avoid that from a biotechnological perspective. We will have moments when our hearts and souls will be broken, because... we are just humans. And that is the truth. That we are created by God in His image, and we are weak and sinful, but Jesus Christ came to earth and saved us, and we are not going to end our lives here in this world, but we will meet the Almighty, with open arms.

Her speech was touching to some people. But most people felt that this speech was offensive, and they felt offended. And they started shouting loudly and clearly that the Murphy sisters didn't deserve to be in this world. And people didn't want their children to even hear about their mad ideas.

Over those few days, the judge and jury seemed to be on the Murphy sisters' side. The judge remembered the old times. The times when this kind of freedom of speech was allowed. He had even heard stories about Martin Luther King from his parents. Nowadays that information was not available anywhere, not in libraries or online. The jury felt similarly, they came from different backgrounds and had different histories. They were touched by the sisters' pure hearts and honesty. They seemed to be good people. And the jury believed them. But during those five days, while the trial was happening, nothing was normal. First there was the live stream, then the global public, and there was no getting away from the outside world for the judge and jury.

They heard people screaming, they had seen people online. They had seen their faces in the newspapers. They knew that they were a part of something bigger. They were unlucky in a way, they couldn't just go with what they were thinking. There was this pressure, which most of them could not handle. The sisters felt that pressure as well. They didn't have any hope that they could win this, but they were calm. They accepted that they would have to suffer, maybe even die. But they felt courage knowing that their parents had done it as well and had shown them how to do it with dignity. Finally, late one evening, around 10 p.m., a decision was made.

'Mary, Helen, Simone and Constance Murphy are guilty of treason and breaking fundamental human rights and we recommend that they be sentenced to death with immediate execution,' read the judge. It was the jury's final decision. He was a bit surprised, but at the same time he knew that a different decision might have started riots and they would all have been in danger.

The girls' faces were sad, but relieved as well. They didn't hope for much anymore, but at least the nightmare was over. Immediate execution meant that they would be injected fairly soon, in the next few days. Just enough time to say goodbye to this world.

They were returned to their prison cell. They didn't talk too much. Each was trying to understand the situation and what would happen in the next few days.

'So this is it, girls! It is over! I'm so sorry!' Helen said and started crying and hugged them all.

'At least we made the crowd happy,' added Conny, smiling.

'It's been a long day and week. Let's get some sleep,' Mary said and went to her bed.

'How do you prepare for death?' They started thinking while lying in bed. Nobody fell asleep quickly. There was too much to digest. 'Could we have done something differently? Does whatever we did actually deserve such cruel punishment?' They were all asking themselves the same questions.

Early the next morning they received a visitor. The judge allowed them to receive family or guests in a more or less unlimited time frame before the execution. This was as much as he could do.
It was Mary's husband, and John, their son. Mary hadn't expected that at all, she was really moved. She spent a few minutes with them.

'I know that I have made mistakes in my life. I hurt people's feelings, and sometimes I did more damage to their lives because of my fantasies. I know that it might not mean much to you, but I'm very sorry for what happened and if I could go back in time I would. I'm so sorry.' Mary started to cry, looking into Eugene's eyes. There was no time for hard feelings anymore. Eugene understood this as well. Tears welled up in his eyes, and he communicated in his own way that he forgave Mary. Mary hugged him. John didn't understand much about what was happening. He was fascinated with the facilities, but didn't really understand why his mum needed to stay in there.

'Mum, why do you have to be here? Why can't you just come home?' John asked.

'Everyone thinks that mum did some awful things, and this meant to be my punishment,' she responded.

'Awful things? Like what? Did you kill somebody? Did you steal something? What did you do?' He was only 6 years old and trying to understand this situation.

'No. I didn't steal anything, or kill anyone. I was trying to save people. But my perception of saving people is not the same as other people's. And perception is understanding …' added Mary to answer the next question.

'Doesn't seem right,' said John after a few seconds of thinking. 'How saving people can deserve punishment. Not sure if I would like to save people,' he added

'Be good to yourself and other people, that will be enough, son.' She smiled and kissed him on the forehead. 'Let me introduce you to someone, I think you met Helen already, and briefly Conny. But I don't think you met Simone yet,' Mary said.

'Hey girls,' she said when she entered their cell. 'John and Eugene are here,' she introduced them and the little boy and his father entered the room.

'I heard so many great things about you,' said Simone straight away and welcomed them. 'Do you know that my son is almost the same age as you?' Simone asked John.

'No, I didn't know. What is his name?' he asked

'Frank!' Simone responded.

'Hello!' Conny called from the back of the cell.

'Great to see you again,' Helen greeted them with a smile.

'Mum, Dad has a message for you,' John suddenly said.

'What message?' Mary asked.

John came to Eugene and took a letter from his pocket and gave it to Mary. She opened it and started reading.

'Oh my,' she said as she turned the page.

'Is everything alright?' Helen asked.

'Yeah, it looks like the UN commissioner got in touch with Eugene and she apologised for what she did to me. She also decided to step down from her position at the UN, and take early retirement to take care of her family,' she summarised the letter.

'Wow, that's a big win for you,' said Conny.

'Helen Murphy!' a guard shouted.

'Yes?' Helen responded.

'There is a phone call for you,' the guard responded and opened the door so she could leave the cell.

'Coming.' Helen left the cell and went to take the phone call.

'Hello, Helen speaking!' she said kindly

'Hi, Mrs Murphy, Jane here,' a young voice responded.

'Hi Jane, how are you?' Helen asked kindly.

'I'm good, thank you. I wanted to apologise. This was not intended. I never in my life thought that this would turn into such a big issue and ruin your life. I feel very bad about that and wanted to ask you for your forgiveness,' Jane said in her young and sad voice.

'I forgive you, Jane. It was not your fault. No one thought that this would grow to be such an issue. You'd better tell me how you are feeling and what you have decided.' Helen tried to cheer her up.

'I'm ok. Had some tough conversations with my father. But I made a decision myself. I want to keep the baby. I know that I'm still very young but well, it happened and we need to live with that. My mum said that she will support me. My dad maybe is not so enthusiastic but still, I made a decision that he respects, so we are good.' Her voice was full of hope.

'Great to hear that. I'm glad that you have worked that out yourself. It is important that you made a decision for yourself.' Helen smiled but Jane could not see it.

'I will have to go now, I have a call with my doctor. I'm sorry that your story is going to end like this. I don't know if I believe in anything, like in God or anything, but please pray for me when you are on the other side, if He exists, of course,' Jane said.

'I will, Jane. Take care and all the best.' Helen was touched by Jane's words.

Helen returned to the cell and told her sisters about Jane's decision. They were happy. It seemed like something good had come of their missions.

'I will miss Frankie so much. It would be so great to see him again. I'm happy that at least you, Mary, were able to see your family,' Simone cried.

'Don't lose hope Simone. Maybe Marcus will bring him so he can say goodbye to you,' Mary added. 'I understand your pain, it was so good to see Eugene and John, and I am relieved that he has forgiven me. I can pass away in peace now.' Mary paused.

'Murphy ladies, you have another guest,' the guard's voice announced.

'Wow, we've got so popular recently,' Conny laughed.

Suddenly, a man wearing red clothes came into the cell. He was smiling and he greeted all the girls personally. He was a priest.

'You wanted a priest. So here I am. My name is O'Sullivan, Father O'Sullivan. We don't have many priests these days, as you probably know the Catholic Church is in a bit of a crisis. I knew your parents personally, I know that you were brought up in the Catholic faith. So I am here to help you with your confession and a final blessing if you wish,' he said and sat down.

'I did ask for the opportunity to talk to a priest, but I didn't expect a cardinal. I'm surprised that my question was even answered, considering the circumstances of why are we here,' Helen said.

'Not sure if your request was fulfilled, I'm here because I wanted to be here. It is not related to this request. I wanted to let you know that our Catholic community has been tracking your trial and obviously they tried to be very supportive through prayer,' he added.

'Nice to hear that!' said Mary. 'If you have a bit of time, could you tell us something about our parents? We have really only heard about them from one side. And we were too young to understand what their beliefs were at the time,' she added.

'Of course. I think I have a bit of time, I did not get any instructions to be honest.' He paused. 'They were amazing people. Very inspiring, even to a priest like me. Priests have more limited possibilities in this world. And even when things got tough in the church, we suffered but at the same time we knew what we had signed up for and it is not easy to change this route for us. For Barb and Nick, it was an everyday struggle. The world was telling them to live their lives differently. To live the way that almost 99% of global society does these days. With no God, or I should say, maybe with ourselves as god. They didn't want to live this way. They wanted to nourish their spiritual lives and to live a deeper life with truth and God.

'They sound not the way I have remembered them, I miss them so much,' Conny said.

'Yes, they were amazing. But it was not an easy life for them. They had to choose every day which way to go. I talked to them many times, and I remember their doubts. I tried to encourage them, and support them as much as I could. They said that it was over for them when they died, but I strongly believe that they are with our Father now, and they are waiting for you. Waiting to welcome you into a better world.

'That all sounds great, but I'm actually very scared and I will miss my son,' said Simone.

'I truly understand what you are saying,' responded Cardinal O'Sullivan. 'Death is a scary thing. It is even worse when you have to leave behind people you love. But we are Christians, we believe that this life is just a part of the path, the journey to meet our Father in heaven. We should not really be afraid, right?' he asked.

'Yeah, sure …' Mary responded. 'It is not as easy as it sounds. I will miss my son and husband, and there are so many things I wanted to see and do but I won't be able to now,' Mary was becoming more and more upset.

'God has a mission for every one of us. Trust Him. He knows what we are capable of, He knows what we can do if we respond to His call. He is leading us to the end of our lives, and bringing us to a new life, in His Kingdom. Have you ever thought about why the saints died, like Saint Dominic or Saint Teresa? They were so good for people and this world. But still

the Lord decided to bring them to the other side.
Why?' he asked.

No one answered, the sisters were just listening.

'Because he loves us so much that he wanted to have those beautiful souls with him already. Because they completed their missions and other people were meant to continue their missions. Like with you. You are here for a reason. This all means something, you are suffering now but when you are on the other side you will be in eternal happiness with the Father. And I'm confident that your death will be a grain planted in many people's hearts, to pick up your missions where you left off, and continue as long as God wants them to be continued,' Cardinal O'Sullivan said.

'Yeah …' Conny said. 'In a way I want to leave this world, seriously. I know, Sis, that you have a lot to live for, life has been treating you well so far. But for me, maybe this mission was the only good thing in my life, and nothing better is likely to happen. And this world … it is so ridiculous. One day they are doing everything to get people to live longer, trying to find cures for diseases, trying to use technology to save our lives. They clone our cells and embryos, help people to live longer and have children. AI doctors can help you anywhere and anytime. Great times for humanity. We can live longer and healthier. At the same time, we abort babies, we use euthanasia to shorten people's lives when it doesn't look the way it should anymore. Soon when all the governments implement the UN regulations, everyone will be able to decide about life and death, just based on quality of life. And we are here, soon to die by injection because someone didn't like what we said and did. Crazy. Deep in my heart, I'm glad we are going to this better world. I think I have never felt at home here …' Conny paused.

'Yes, this is not our motherland,' added Cardinal O'Sullivan.

'But how is my life and what I did a grain of goodness for others? Why? I did not do anything spectacular or anything. Even more, I didn't even complete my mission,' said Helen

'Not one of us actually completed her mission, to be fair,' Simone added

'Yeah, exactly! How is this worth anything, tell me! I was a failure my whole life. Didn't do anything that is worth mentioning by historians.' Helen was upset.

'Hmm … yeah, I know what you mean but this is exactly what God does, He takes things with his hands and turns them into goodness and love, which inspires the next generation. Your actions won't be forgotten, believe me. They will try to clear the whole internet, but there will still be people who will keep your words and actions in their hearts and only God has access to humans' hearts,' he said

'Again, the cardinal is very knowledgeable and wise, but this doesn't speak to my heart …' Helen answered.

'Let me say it this way, then. Not sure if you remember this place: Rome and the Vatican, in Italy. This was the home for Catholic popes for centuries. As you probably know, it is not like that anymore. I went there once, with my mum, for her sixtieth birthday. We had a great time, I really enjoyed it. But when I was in Saint Peter's Basilica I had these thoughts about the meaning of our life in the context of the history of humankind. You could see all of those altars in the basilica, dedicated to different popes. The same in the Vatican Grottoes, where they keep the relics of popes from different centuries. Popes, they were the leaders of the Catholic Church, they took care of the poor and suffering in this world, they took care of art and many other things. Of course they were the successors of St Peter, they held the keys to heaven …' He paused. 'But pilgrims, people visiting that place … they didn't even stop and pray at those altars. They were passing by. They were stopping by to see the Pietà, or paintings in the Sistine Chapel by Michelangelo. And he was just an artist, from the sixteenth century. But his work survived so many centuries. This was extraordinary work, touched by God. No one before or after did anything similar. AI would not be able to replicate that, because you need a heart and soul to do it,' the cardinal said.

'And how is that similar to our story?' Helen asked.

'The most important thing is not what you have done but your approach, your heart and soul are the most important things. At the end of the day what matters is what they will remember about you. For example Jane, is she will remember that you tried to help her. You came to her like Christ would, and gave her your helping hand,' he finished.

Cardinal O'Sullivan was able to give them a blessing and listen to their confessions before he was asked to leave the cell.

The next couple of days were quiet. No more visitors, no more thoughts. Just silence for most of the day. They were trying to make peace with themselves. And their day came. It was delayed for different reasons, but it was eventually scheduled for Friday, 3 p.m. sharp.

The girls put on the best clothes they had. Conny said, smiling: 'Let's say goodbye to this life in style.' They put a little make up on just to highlight the beauty of their faces. It was just enough. They looked astonishing. People who cheered for them had tears in their eyes when they saw them coming to the execution room. The people who wanted them to die were saying, 'such a pity that those beautiful women have to die because of their dangerous and toxic ideologies'.

It was different from usual. One thing was that it is very rare to have four people going to the execution room together. The death penalty in general is a very rare punishment, and usually there is only one person on the chair. This time they had four. They had to redesign the room so they could fit all of them and ensure that it would be possible to show it on TV and stream it online. The demand to see those girls killed was huge, and the global village couldn't miss out on this opportunity to earn billions of dollars.

Another thing that was different this time was the absence of family members. Obviously they couldn't count on their parents because they had passed away already, or rather they had been killed. But no one else showed up. It was not the best time to show that you were a part of that cursed Murphy family.

The execution performance started at 3 p.m. as planned. People from the court started reading the sentence and justification for the death penalty. In the meantime, the girls entered and sat down on the chairs. They were given some tablets so they wouldn't go into shock when the poison was injected. Then there was a commercial break so the organisers of the whole event could cash in on those five billion viewers. The whole thing was directed like a TV show. Each sister was injected with the poison separately. And there was a commercial break after each was injected. They started with Mary, followed by Helen, Simone and Conny. Conny saw them all die.

When the poison was injected into Mary, and the commercials started playing, Helen said to the girls beside her, 'His face looks familiar'. She was looking at the man who was injecting the poison. 'Or maybe it is just those tablets they gave us.'

'Wow, Helen … you didn't say that you have friends who work in the execution room,' Simone replied. 'And this jerk is even smiling while doing it, what an asshole!' Conny didn't find it funny.

Considering the circumstances they were in, they were very calm. It was like this internal peace that they had was spreading around them, and no storm outside could change their wellbeing. Because maybe it is not circumstances that create or destroy our peace but the fact that we are doing something that goes against our conscience. Perhaps that is the main thing that kills peace in our souls.

When the executioner got to Conny, something happened. Something five billion people were waiting for. Conny got mad and started screaming, crying and laughing. She lost her mind watching her sisters dying. It was painful to watch. Hurtful. But they played commercials so people could not complain about the disturbing pictures.

And then they were gone. They were history and the whole world could live their happy lives again. That dangerous ideology, those scary criminals, had been eliminated. The world was at peace again and could sleep easy. The TV stations were counting their profits and quietly hoping for more cases like this. But as is the case with every human life that goes, the world was not the same anymore. It couldn't be.

13

'Where is Mummy?' Frank asked his father, Marcus.

'She is gone, my son, she passed away,' Marcus responded quickly without giving it much thought.

'But why? Was she sick?' Frank continued digging.

'No, she wasn't. It was just her time to leave this place and move somewhere else,' Marcus responded, trying to give him a bit more hope with his response.

'Where? Where did she go?' Frank asked

'I don't know, son,' Marcus replied.

Frank was quiet for almost the whole day, like he was thinking about something. Maybe about these questions and answers about Mum. He kept doing normal things, but he didn't look too enthusiastic about them, like he normally would be. He didn't understand what 'passing away' really meant. And that 'other place', bothered him. Would his mum be willing to leave him and go somewhere else? And why?

'You know, Dad,' he suddenly said during dinner. 'I don't know why Mummy left for somewhere else, but I feel that something is wrong here, and I'm sad. I loved her. She loved me, she gave me everything she could I guess. And now she is just gone, and I'm alone,' he finished.

'You are not alone, you have me,' Marcus interrupted.

'Yeah, I have you. But Mum was important too, I think. It is hard to explain. I feel really sad and lonely.' Frank added.

Marcus didn't respond to that last sentence. He probably felt something similar. It hadn't worked out between him and Simone, but at the same time they had been married for a few years and there had been some kind of intimacy that had bonded them. This wasn't the only thing. Something had started changing in the world after that execution. There was more fear about people's lives. People were discouraged from thinking for themselves. All the information they were getting was personalised, tailored perfectly to their needs, so they didn't have to search for anything. A fear of dangerous ideologies had also pushed the UN, the EU and global governments, along with tech companies and international secret intelligence services, to work together and create one global government that was led by three people who represented three of the most powerful nations in the world: China, the US, and Russia. In their first announcement just a month after the execution of the Murphy sisters they declared:

Global nations have developed humanity to this stage, where everyone is truly free and can be him/her/itself. All people are accepted no matter what

Very quickly after that announcement, global governments started changing their laws so they could imprison and execute those who were a threat to humanity. If local governments were opposed to the idea, they immediately lost their connections to the global economy and these governments were replaced very quickly in the next election by unhappy voters.

Weeks later when you walked on the street, you saw all of those happy people. Smiling, being good to each other, helping each other. This seemed like a paradise on earth. People were happy because they were told to be happy. And if they didn't feel happy they were given medicine to feel happy. You couldn't be sure if AI had gone down one level of development or if humanity had gone one level up, but you could not tell the difference between who was a human and who was a robot.

Everything seemed to be fake, but that was the new reality. Everything was planned, designed. Every aspect of being a human was organised from start to the finish. There were no more spontaneous actions, love now meant happiness, and happiness was just a feeling you had when your belly was full, and you felt pleasure when someone gave you a massage.

After this short but very meaningful discussion with his son, Marcus thought a lot about what he had done to his relationship with Simone. He thought about how it was possible that she had been such a good mother. Her absence had left a hole in Frank's heart. He was not the same kid as he had been before. Marcus was suffering as well, he had many regrets because of Simone. But he could not forget the words that Frank had said to him, they resonated in him for much longer; his role as a father meant more to him now.

'Frank, tell me, how can I be a better father to you?' he suddenly asked his son.

'I don't know Dad, Mum would probably know … but she is not here anymore,' he answered sadly.

Marcus didn't have a choice, he had to find a way to become a good father. He started spending more time with Frank, hoping to build a relationship with him that was as close as the one he had had with Simone. But building relationships wasn't his strong suit. It was not a strong suit for many people those days. The world looked totally connected, everyone was constantly online, but at the same time people were so far from each other. Years later, when online identification was introduced, people lived only in this realm of virtual reality where they could be whoever they wanted, look the way they wanted and do whatever they wished for.

It seemed like AI, and technological developments over the past few decades, had left people without the skill of talking to people in reality, and the capacity to build deep relationships. Those days were gone. People were only active on social media, where everyone in the world could see your posts and read your opinions.

This was a new era of human development, an era without deep feelings. Our animal instincts started to be treated as our natural way of behaving, the real us, the reality of satisfying human needs was seen as the ultimate goal of our existence.

And we could end this story here. The Murphy sisters were gone, but that was not the end of the story. The bodies of the Murphy sisters had been collected by Mr John Arymatovich. He was the owner of a funeral company in New York State. None of their family members had attended the sisters' execution. Obviously Eugene and John could have been there, but Eugene decided that he preferred to spend this time somewhere else with his son. They had already said their goodbyes to Mary.
After the execution, Eugene was the only family member who decided to do something with the Murphy sisters' bodies. He wanted to have a standard Catholic funeral for them. It was not easy to find Mr Arymatovich. He was the only one who

responded to Eugene's request. Other funeral homes were simply too busy, or maybe they just didn't want to do it because of the publicity.

The standard process for those kinds of executions was that, first of all, the doctors checked if the person was actually dead. At the time it was much easier to check this. Most people had a chip under their skin that was used as ID, a payment method and also to monitor human health parameters like their heart rate and so on. Prison data analysts quickly connected to the chips after the execution and checked the functionality of the sisters' internal organs.

'They are gone!' they happily announced.

John Arymatovich was then invited to come inside and he directed other people to remove the bodies from the chairs, pack them into special bags and put them into his car. Then he drove to his funeral home, where he wanted to prepare the bodies for the funeral, which was already planned for the next day. He put each body on the table, cleaned it, and embalmed it. He hibernated body parts so they would last longer. Later on, some of the organs would be used for different purposes. This was a standard procedure that had been introduced all over the world a few years back. The clothes still looked great so he left them as they were. He removed all the chips, and deleted the entries from the global identification system that had been introduced for people's safety because of terrorist attacks. The sisters were officially gone from this world.

14

Eugene, the only close family member who had not been afraid to be present during the trial, also took care of the funeral arrangements. Of course Eugene himself needed help with day-to-day things, so he was really not able to organise it himself. But his will was there, and that was enough.

Surprisingly Eugene and John received some help during the trial. One day, a middle-aged lady showed up at Eugene's apartment and said that from now on she would take care of him and John.

Eugene was so shocked that he didn't really ask why. He was just happy that someone would be with them and would take care of things. It was pretty difficult for him to take care of himself, never mind John's needs.

That lady, whose name was Maria, was an experienced caretaker and childminder. She was very quick to take up new duties and she didn't take no for an answer. Interestingly enough, she was not paid by Mary, as Eugene thought at the start. Months later he discovered that she was paid by a woman from the UN who Mary had dealt with. He didn't know if this was just a gesture of love and care, or if this woman had some regrets in relation to what had happened to Mary. It didn't matter, really, so he didn't look into this for a long time. He was happy that they had some help, finally. Maria also helped Eugene with the funeral. This was not the easiest task, given that no one wanted to be associated with the Murphy family. It was definitely not the most popular surname at the time. But Maria was a very skilful person, and based on the instructions she got from Eugene she was able to organise a funeral home, priest and other things that were required by law.

The idea was to organise a funeral very quickly, everyone wanted it to be over as soon as possible. Maria got everyone lined up pretty well. The bodies were prepared for the funeral and all their identifying details were removed from the global identification systems. The next day Maria and Eugene went over to the funeral parlour to see if everything was ready. On the way back from the funeral home, they visited a small parish in the Bronx.

The priest from that parish, 75-year-old Irish priest Seamus O'Burke, was really the only one who was happy to celebrate the Eucharist at the funeral. They had a quick chat about the ceremony itself, and what they were planning to say during the Mass.

The funeral itself started very late, compared to the usual time for those kinds of events. It started at 8 p.m. on Saturday. Not many people attended the Mass in the small chapel at the cemetery. Only Eugene and John represented the Murphy family. There were some friends who were not afraid of governments, or who just didn't care. Saying goodbye to close friends was more important to them than avoiding problems with the police or the FBI.

The funerals looked very different from how they had years back. Most people now signed up to donate their organs after their death. All the information was stored in the global identification system. When the chips were removed from the sisters' skin on their arms, all information about the state of their health and their internal organs had also been transferred to the system. In return, the system was able to identify organs that were needed by patients right then, or which organs would be needed for scientific research. The same thing happened during the analysis of the sisters' health. The only thing was that even though sisters were pretty healthy, their organs had been removed from the donor list automatically because of 'other concerns'.

The concept was that after the funeral ceremony at the cemetery, only symbolic possessions belonging to the person who had passed away would be kept in the ground. The coffins were brought back to the funeral home, where the next step in the process could happen.

The Eucharistic celebration went pretty smoothly. The chapel was half empty, so there was not much excitement or despair. It is worth mentioning that all of the funeral arrangements had been kept secret so that random people would not come over to protest and shout offensive slogans at the mourners.

After the Mass, the procession moved to the cemetery. This cemetery was not big. The graves were pretty small, the place was even a bit too full. The graves were close to each other, there was not much space to stand, never mind sit anywhere. The procession went around the whole cemetery. The weather was good. It was still bright, but dusk was just around the corner. There was no wind so the whole procession was not rushed at all. The coffins were transported on special electric vans that were the standard mode of transport in those days. Some people who had been in the chapel decided not to go with the procession. Perhaps they were just afraid. Or maybe it was too much for them from an emotional point of view.

The graves were in the north-west corner of the cemetery. This was not the most luxurious spot in the cemetery. There were plenty of bushes, the grass hadn't been cut and there was loads of rubbish. Maria tried to clean it up before the funeral but she hadn't had much time. It had been pretty difficult to get this space in this cemetery at all and this was the only corner they were allowed to use.

During the funeral ceremony, only a few people stood around the grave and coffins. Some journalists were seen behind trees. During the ceremony, Maria read a letter from Eugene, as he was obviously unable to read it himself or even express how he felt. Maria had made a note of his thoughts over the last few days since the jury verdict had been announced. She also added a few sentences from little John who, despite having been adopted by Mary and Eugene, really felt strongly bonded with his new Mum and Dad.

Eventually Father O'Burke had something to say. It was very touching and emotional for the people who heard it: 'When God created a woman from Adam's rib, he called her to be a 'help' to man. The Bible uses a very specific word for this, which later will be used by Jewish people when they seek a special intervention from God. That would mean that God created Eve as an essential part of man's life. Over centuries we could see that. As much as men seemed to be physically stronger than women, and to hold all the power in their hands, because they could hunt and get food to support their families, they were still very dependent on women's help.

'Women were always able to organise important parts of life that men were never able to. When we look at the history of humankind, we can see that women always took care of the most important parts of being human. Building relationships with people, taking care of vulnerable people, giving birth to every human. Their role is essential in humanity's history, though it was never properly appreciated. And it is not a case of equality. That should be obvious to anyone. Equal pay – that concerns women doing the same type of jobs as men, no question about that, but they still bring something new to the table. Women and men are not the same, they were designed by God for a different purpose, so their characters are different and that's good. Very good. Humanity would not survive if we did not have men or women in this world, with everything that they bring to this world.

'The Murphy sisters brought to this world their specific features. The Bible often uses the word "goodness" as a synonym for the word "beautiful" and that's what this is really about. The most beautiful women in the history of humankind were not models, or celebrities who changed their looks with plastic surgery, or just women who have loads of makeup on. Real beauty comes from inside. From their hearts. From being good. We men have all experienced meeting those kinds of women, who might not be very young anymore, and may not be wearing the nicest dresses, but they have this divine element in them that makes them special, they are "full of grace".

'Those words, used by the angel who met Mary, give us this idea, about women who are full of grace, full of this beautiful goodness in their hearts that shines through them and out onto other people. That is a mystical gift. We cannot fully understand that gift; we cannot phrase it so it can be taken in by the human brain. We can just see how it has affected humankind over the centuries.

'And now, we are looking at the graves of four young sisters. I never met them personally, but I have no doubt that they had this divine element in them as well. When you look at their story, you can wonder why they changed their lives so dramatically. They left behind what they had, their jobs, in a way their families, as well, and started working on some missions that are not understood at all by 80% of society anymore. So why did they do it? Because something in their hearts was telling them that the truth lies somewhere else. They felt that they needed to intervene in this world again, because their families and humankind were in danger. They were willing to sacrifice everything they had, even their lives, for this purpose.'

Some people started to leave while Father O'Burke was still talking. Maybe they disagreed with his thoughts, but most likely they were just afraid and didn't want to be linked with this event and these people after all. The ceremony finished just before 9 p.m. Father O'Burke came to Eugene and John, shook their hands and passed on his condolences to the whole family. After that everyone went back to their homes and the bodies were transported back to the funeral home, where the next step – recovering the organs – was meant to be taken.

It was already late when the coffins were delivered to the funeral home. The recovery of organs was meant to start the following day, on Sunday morning. The bodies were removed from the wooden coffins and put back into the cooler. The lights were turned off and everyone went home. Around 8 a.m. the following day, something strange happened. One of the bodies in the plastic bags moved. Over time it started moving more and more, and finally one of the hands made a hole in the bag. It was Mary. For some reason she was alive. She opened the bag and slowly got out of it. She looked very confused.

'It is very cold here,' she said quietly, her teeth chattering. 'Where am I?' she thought. It took her a few minutes to fully regain consciousness. She was not really familiar with funeral stores, so she didn't understand where she was. When she started looking around she realised that one of her sisters had also started moving in the next bag. She quickly went over to her table and helped her to open the bag. It was Helen.

'I'm so glad that I can see you again,' Mary cried out.

'Hey, sister.' Helen was in shock. 'Where are we?' She started looking around.

'No idea, to be honest, but it is pretty cold,' Mary responded.

Simone and Constance woke up a few minutes later as well. They all looked the same at the start; they were shocked and didn't really know where they were.

'Is this a new world or something? Looks pretty dull,' Constance said

'I think it is still our old world,' responded Mary.

'Can we get out of here, I will freeze to death otherwise,' said Simone

'Not sure if you can be more dead than we were,' Constance laughed.

'Yeah, true. Is there any way out?' Simone asked.

'We tried different options, it looks like the doors are closed from the outside so it won't be easy to open them,' Mary responded.

'So what are we going to do?' said Simone. It was 9 a.m. already. 'I don't know if we can survive this cold for much longer,' she added

For the next ten minutes all of them looked for things to either cover themselves with or to change the temperature. No one really keeps blankets in the morgue, so they were unsuccessful. Mary, though, was able to find the temperature controls, but of course they were mostly operated by an app and an AI-powered device, but she was able to hack into it and change the temperature. Obviously she couldn't turn it up as high as she wished to, but she was able to raise it from 40 degrees to a more comfortable temperature for everyone. They spent the next few hours thinking about what to do next, about where they were and why they were alive. Just before 1 p.m. Constance said: 'I'm actually hungry. I thought that I wouldn't feel any hunger in this new world.' She smiled.

'Me too, I could eat a big fat burger right now,' Simone commented.

'We were dead for some time, I guess, there is no reason why we wouldn't be hungry, but I don't think this is a place where we can get something to eat,' Mary said, looking around.

'Fair point Mary, I would prefer to not even look for food here,' Helen added.

Around 1 p.m. they heard a noise outside the door.

'Listen, be quiet, I think someone is outside,' Mary said quietly. They hid in the corner, behind some beds. The door opened and a middle-aged man in a New York Knicks cap entered the room, smiled, and said: 'Hello girls, anybody hungry?'

'Helen stood up straight, looked at him and responded, 'Dad? Is it really you?' She was sure it was him. She started running towards him. The girls followed her. He opened his arms, and Helen jumped into them to hug him. The rest of the girls got to him quickly and hugged him as well.

'Good to have you back, I missed you so much,' he said.

Helen and Mary were really excited and happy to see him, it seemed like the anger they had felt in the past was gone. It was a bit different with Conny and Simone. They had worked out those feelings in their hearts, or maybe tried to escape from them. Now was the time to confront them once and for all. They turned their heads and the battle in their hearts started.

15

'So, tell us! Where are we? What happened?' Simone asked when they sat down.

'How come the last thing we saw was the execution room, and now we are here? Is this a new life?' Mary asked.

'By the way … was it you? In the execution room?' Helen asked, looking into his eyes.

'Girls, I know that you are very excited about this whole situation. So many questions, I will answer them all. But slowly. We have time. I brought some food, I know that you are starving.' They moved to another room.

'I don't think that eating sandwiches in the morgue is the most enjoyable, so let's sit here.' He sat down on a chair. The girls followed him. He opened some boxes with sandwiches.

'So how come we are still alive?' Simone asked again.

'Because I injected you with a fake poison. It lasts for about forty-eight hours. It reduces your heartbeat to the minimum so that you seem to be dead. And so you are dead to this world. Your records have been erased. Even the master data, I checked this morning.' He smiled.

'What is the master data?' Mary asked.

'Usually governments record some very generic data about people to identify them. But there is more and more data about people, mostly because of the chips that everyone has under their skin. Master data seems to be very complex and to have expanded recently, so many more events from people's lives are noted. But …' he paused. 'In your case it is a bit different. Governments know that there is no data in this world that cannot be stolen, so the only way to prevent this is to properly wipe it. Your trial, your beliefs are not something this government or whoever has power in this world wants to actually keep, so it will be gone soon, if it isn't already.' He smiled

'Ok. So that means that we don't exist within the structure of this world,' Mary added.

'Yes, that's correct,' he answered.

'But how are you alive, we saw you being killed? What about Mum?' Helen asked.

'Mum is alive as well. We are sort of hiding. To be honest, we don't really need to hide. There is no evidence of us living in this world so no one really cares. There are another nine billion people they need to worry about,' Dad said.

'But how did that happen? How did you survive?' Constance asked.

'Well, it was just a fake death, a fake execution … similar to yours. We have our tricks,' he said

'We? Are there more people like you?' Simone asked

'Yes, there are many more of us. All of those the world wants to forget about, because they don't like what they believe in or what they do and say,' Nick said.

'Wow, that sounds interesting. How are you able to live here undercover?' Mary asked

'We have our methods and ideas. We are still trying to ignite the world with our beliefs …' he paused. 'Are you done with your food?' he asked politely. 'Let's go and see Mum now.'

'Mum! I can't wait to see her,' Constance responded excitedly.

They drove in a car that was not self-driving. It was the opposite, even, there were no electronics in it, so the car was not traceable. They left New York and came to a small village, there weren't many houses. Nothing interesting was happening there. There was just this old factory that looked abandoned.

'Here we are,' he said.

'Do you really live here? It looks abandoned,' Helen said.

'That's the whole point! No one really cares about places like this. Maps are not updated, because we are not connected to anything, it does not show up in any systems,' he responded before they stopped.

'Amazing!' Simone replied.

He drove the car into the building and they parked close to windows. There were some other vehicles there as well, not only cars. They looked around when they got out of the car. It didn't really look like a place from 2037. No 'smart' systems, no electronics at all, really. The place looked empty. But not for too long.

'Let me give you a tour,' Dad said.

'Cool. Can't wait,' said Mary, who was the most impressed with the whole place. They entered another hall through a huge iron door. It was not so quiet and empty out there. So this is where we keep our food!' Nick exclaimed.

'How come? Where?' Conny was disoriented.

'You see the greenhouses over there, in the corner? In a way this is the only place here where we use a bit of technology. Biotechnology, to be exact. Nature is not producing a lot these days, because we humans have destroyed most of our natural habitat. We don't really eat meat either, so we try to have a balanced, efficient diet,' he added

'Sounds interesting. Yeah, the food these days is far from what I had when I was little,' Mary responded.

'Yeah, I don't really remember any other food,' Conny said.

'You can't really, we almost killed the earth in the 2020s,' Dad replied.

'You can look at beautiful old pictures and footage of our planet on TV today … and that's it, really,' Helen said.

They walked through the hall. The sisters were looking around at everything, at the place where their parents were living. It felt surreal.

'Is there anyone else living here besides you and Mum? I know you mentioned something like that already,' Simone asked.

'Yes, you will meet all of them. There are about forty people living here. But there are some other places in the US and globally, in other countries as well, where the same thing applies. People who are not needed by humanity anymore. So they are removed from the system, from life, in a way, and live in these ghettos,' he answered.

'Oh, do you talk to each other? In those different places? Or maybe you meet?' Simone followed up.

'We can't really meet if it involves using airplanes as a mode of transportation. That's a really closely monitored way of moving around. You can't really get on a plane if there is no record of you in the system' he answered.

'Makes sense. If you hacked the system and were discovered then they would trace you. So how do you communicate with other folks? How do you even buy petrol for your cars?' Mary asked.

'We use the dark web to communicate. We use it for many other things as well. With money it is a bit simpler. Blockchain technology has made that very easy and pretty much anonymous. So we have no problems with buying petrol or other things, but in most cases we try to get stuff ourselves. Grow some plants. We pay for our internet connection, but again this happens via blockchain payment systems,' Dad answered.

'Amazing. Is the dark web a good place to be?' Helen asked.

'We saw Dad's video there,' Conny commented.

'True, the only place really where we could see it,' Helen said.

'Which video, the one at the United Nations?' Dad asked.

'Yes, do you have more?' Helen asked

'Yeah kind of, that is actually the work we are doing. We try to keep those things somewhere on the web. We put that video there, the same as hundreds of others. Also books, music and other stuff that keeps people alive in some way. The dark web is not as bad as it used to be. It is bad for the world, but it contains everything that governments don't want to share,' he said.

'What do you mean, keeps people alive?' Simone asked while they were passing through another iron gate.

'Yeah, you see, in some ways the world is full of great things, people, and technology. At the same time, inside, people are just dead. There is nothing more for them than the current world. We are trying to ignite their hearts again,' Dad responded.

The next hall looked a bit different. There were tents around the whole place.

'So you are living in the tents?' Mary asked.

'Kind of. These are really good tents, Mary, not like the ones you used when you were in the Scouts when you were a kid.' He paused. 'Look who is coming our way,' he pointed to a woman who was coming towards him. She was smiling.

'Hello girls,' Barb said. 'So good to have you back.' She started hugging them, they were all smiling and crying at the same time.

'Mummy, we missed you so much,' Helen shouted with tears in her eyes.

'Come to the dining room, I have prepared some cookies and tea,' she said and led all of them to a special room. They sat down in this small room and Mum brought them some cookies that she had baked herself.

'These are so good, Mum,' Constance said.

'I'm glad you like them! I have been waiting for this moment for so long!' She got emotional as well and hugged her again. 'You are so big now, Conny!' she added.

'Dad, I have a question for you, was that your voice in the attic? Did the missions come from you?' Mary asked curiously.

'Yes, that was my voice. The missions came from both of us. To be frank, we monitored your lives. We knew exactly what was happening. We decided that you needed this and we figured that those missions and our old house would bring you all back together,' Dad said.

'We knew about your personal problems, we knew about what happened to Helen, and to Simone at home. We knew about Mary's husband's accident. We knew how Conny's life was messed up. And we decided that it was time to start this. We didn't want to lose you,' she added.

'Incredible, but I threw out the letter, it was just pure luck that I happened to be in that neighbourhood,' Conny said.

'Was it?' Dad smiled. 'Conny, your letter was blank, because we knew that you would throw it away. But at the same time, we knew that you wouldn't pass up the opportunity to go to that party in our old neighbourhood.' He smiled again.

'That's crazy, how much information you could get, even being outside of the system,' Mary said.

'Information is not everything. I guess some corporations, secret intelligence services have more information than we could get. But the key here was to know your hearts. To know who you really are,' Dad added.

'I know that you might be sad that you left your families behind there. I understand. You can still help them, from here. They won't know that it is you, but you can still ignite their hearts and in some way lead them through this life. So don't worry,' Barb said.

'Thanks Mum, I really worry about Frank,' Simone said.

'Don't worry. I will show you something. We have access to your home cameras in Boston,' Dad said. They stood up and went to another room. This room was very impressive. A bit like a NASA command centre. There were many monitors, a bit of equipment, many different things.

'Amazing!' Mary shouted. 'I can't believe that you are not traceable with all of this gear here,' she added and started looking around. 'The amount of heat this is producing, I'm sure that survelllance cameras can see this with infrared cameras.'

'Not really, if you have a good cooling system or special cover walls and a roof,' he winked at her.

'Even more amazing!' Mary exclaimed.

'I'm already overwhelmed by this,' Simone said.

'Don't worry honey, I feel the same sometimes,' Mum said to her and kissed her. 'Let me just show you a recent video from your house,' she said and started searching for it on the computer.

'Still, you don't have the newest technology,' Mary remarked with a smile and winked at Dad.

'Well, all that new stuff is so easy to track. Not sure what bubble you were living in, my software wizard, but pretty much all of the components in today's electronic devices have traceable pieces,' he replied with a smile and hugged her.

Barb showed Simone the video of her husband talking to Frank. She had tears in her eyes.
'I know honey, it is touching. You see, your decision might have had more of an impact than you think,' she said as she smiled at her.

Later that evening they decided to light a fire in the fireplace. Years back they had really loved sitting around the fireplace, singing, eating marshmallows and having fun together. Some memories came back.

'You have died for this world. You were reborn to a new life,' Barb started. 'Not really eternal life, that is yet to come, but life in Christ. Here on earth already. You might think that all of that was worthless. But you have planted a seed in people's hearts. You did something extraordinary. That won't go away. Also, this is not about Mum or Dad, it is about your own relationship with God and how it defines you. This is not the end, this is just the start of a new life,' she finished and grabbed her guitar. 'Let's sing some old-school songs,' she said and started playing.

She played a few songs that were well known, but maybe not for the sisters, because it had been a while since they had actually done something like this. But it was nice, they were relaxed and relieved. They felt happy. They felt that this was just the beginning of a new life. Their new missions had just begun.

'Dad?' Helen interrupted one of the songs. 'We know what you were doing, we know everything about this life here. But when did you actually start thinking about this, this way? When did you decide to start this new underground life?' she asked.

'Well, I remember when this little rebel moved out,' he smiled at Mary. 'I started having some discussions with your mum about the situation, and about how we wanted to raise our daughters. We knew that eventually something bad would happen to us, and we just prepared for that moment. Obviously we didn't control all of it, and we didn't choose the timing. It was not our plan to leave Constance when she was only 13 years old …we did not know what would happen after we were gone. We hoped that the family would take care of you, but we were mistaken. We are sorry that this is how everything worked out. But to briefly answer your question: yes, everything started with Mary …'